Praise for *Level Up or Die*, Joshua Lisec, and Adam Lane Smith

"[*Level Up or Die* is a] blunt, fast-moving, entertaining tale set in a steampunk virtual reality world."
— *Kirkus Reviews*

"Joshua Lisec started at an early age, gives all the best tips on how to get started, makes a great living, and you can as well."
— James Altucher
Wall Street Journal Bestselling Author,
Choose Yourself and *The Power of No*
Host, *The James Altucher Show*

"Joshua Lisec is an expert on ghostwriting and getting published. Talk to him. You know you're getting expert advice from somebody who's done it a number of times."
— Scott Adams
Dilbert Creator, *New York Times* Bestselling Author,
Loserthink and *Win Bigly*

"Joshua Lisec is the #1 ghostwriter in the world."
— Ed Latimore
Bestselling Author, Retired Professional Boxer

"Adam Lane Smith seamlessly blends genres like he's been doing it forever."
— Rhett C. Bruno
Bestselling Author of The Circuit Trilogy

Also by Joshua Lisec

The Phoenix Reich
The Compass

Also by Adam Lane Smith

Gideon Ira: Knight of the Blood Cross
Gideon Ira and the Winter Valkyrie
Gideon Ira in Castle Bloodghast
Valkyrie Doll and the Ashen Brotherhood
Making Peace
Savage Hunters
Maxwell Cain: Burrito Avenger
Maxwell Cain 2: With a Side of Vengeance

LEVEL UP OR DIE,

VOLUME 1

*"You guys are nuts. You really should cut and run.
Anyone else would."*

"Sure. But who wants to be normal?"

LEVEL UP OR DIE

A LITRPG STEAMPUNK ADVENTURE

VOLUME 1

JOSHUA LISEC

ADAM LANE SMITH

The Entrepreneur's
Wordsmith LLC

The Entrepreneur's Wordsmith LLC
Beavercreek, Ohio

The Entrepreneur's Wordsmith LLC

The Entrepreneur's Wordsmith LLC
Beavercreek, Ohio
www.EntrepreneursWordsmith.com
Joshua@EntrepreneursWordsmith.com

Publisher's Cataloging-In-Publication Data

Names: Lisec, Joshua, author. | Smith, Adam Lane, 1985- author.
Title: Level up or die : a LitRPG steampunk adventure / Joshua Lisec [and] Adam Lane Smith.
Description: Beavercreek, Ohio : The Entrepreneur's Wordsmith LLC, [2021] | Series: Level up or die ; volume 1
Identifiers: ISBN 9781737181507 (softcover paperback) | ISBN 9781737181514 (jacketed case laminate hardcover) | ISBN 9781737181521 (Kindle ebook)
Subjects: LCSH: Fantasy games--Fiction. | Electronic games--Fiction. | Political corruption--Fiction. | Political prisoners--Fiction. | Families--Fiction. | LCGFT: Steampunk fiction. | Political fiction.
Classification: LCC PS3612.I81 L48 2021 (print) | LCC PS3612.I81 (ebook) | DDC 813/.6--dc23

To every son who hopes to make his father proud.

CONTINUE THE ADVENTURE

Be the first to hear about *Level Up or Die*, Volume 2 and other novels, nonfiction, short stories, and courses by Joshua Lisec and Adam Lane Smith. Here's how.

- Subscribe to Joshua and Adam's literary newsletter at www. LisecAndSmithBooks.com.
- Visit Joshua's website at www.EntrepreneursWordsmith.com.
- Check out Adam's blog at www.AdamLaneSmith.com.
- Follow Joshua (@JoshuaLisec) and Adam (@The-Brometheus) on Twitter.

Introducing *The 80/20 Fiction System*

Write a Great Novel Faster Than You Ever Thought Possible

The novel you're about to read was produced using Joshua Lisec and Adam Lane Smith's *80/20 Fiction System*. Crafted from years of experience writing a combined total of 80 books, this program leverages the 80/20 Principle so you invest time on only activities that produce a commercially viable book — and none on activities that don't.

If you've always wanted to write a novel, or if you're an author looking to crank your productivity into overdrive, check out Joshua and Adam's fiction writing masterclass at **www.8020FictionSystem.com**.

CONTENTS

CHAPTER 1

INTO THE COFFIN

"**D**onovan Riley, you have been found guilty of manslaughter."
My hog of a judge pauses for dramatic effect. The crusty-eyed mouth breathers packing the stadium seats wheeze and applaud.

Shame they don't sell popcorn. They'd make a killing.

I can't even guess how many people are livestreaming the trial at home. Camera drones swarm around my sister's bloody bedroom as the replay flickers above the court pit. In that frozen nightmare, I'm standing at her bedside over a man's crumpled body. Gore mats my dark hair. The only way to avoid the hologram is to bow my head. It's what these clowns want, but I can't face my shame.

One drone buzzes down for a money shot of my public pretender, Johnny Garcia. He flashes a bleached grin for his closeup. "Smile for the folks at home, Donny boy. Better a high-rated convict than a free nobody."

"Who gives a shit about ratings, man? The folks at home gonna take care of my mom and sis?"

"Silence!" the bloated judge says. The two chrome-suited bailiffs who chained me to the defendant's table approach from both sides to drag me out of the pit. Whistles, jeers, and boos erupt from the stands.

"I'll take care of your mom!" some drunk shouts from the box seats.

Mom and Sis are up there somewhere in the nosebleeds. I can't bear to look for them. They're probably crying.

"Mr. Riley!" His Portliness gavels the spectators to silence. "Any last words before your sentence?"

I straighten up to my full height, which isn't much at five eight, but screw you. "I did the right thing. My conscience is clear."

The judge peers down his long nose like I'm a bug in his soup. "Public safety drones literally caught you red-handed, Mr. Riley. I'd hoped some time in your cell might instill a little decency. Instead, you show this court the same aggression your history of street violence suggests."

"Anyone in my position would have done exactly what I did. Even a bloated warthog like you."

The audience gasps.

"First manslaughter, now fatphobia." The judge's eyes bulge.

Hope they pop like microwaved eggs. That would be a riot.

"Given the . . . complex nature of your case, Mr. Riley, I was inclined to show leniency. Instead, I feel only the maximum sentence will do. Your constitutional rights are hereby suspended. As punishment for your crime, you shall serve a period of no less than fifteen years in the Games."

The audience howls with glee. The drones swivel to grab reaction shots for the holoscreen behind the judge's throne. A chick in a green tube top squeezes her boobs for the camera.

A slender blonde in a purple neon bikini replaces the live feed. A golden sash slung over her ample chest reads *Rachel Justice, California's Favorite Sentencing AI™*.

Silence blankets the court as spectators shush each other.

"Congratulations, defendant," Rachel says. "You've just been sentenced to a thrilling adventure in *God's Staircase*, the newest correctional tower game brought to you by Cryoblend Corp. Inside, you'll discover adventures untold. Just be careful not to get hooked—you just might stay there for life!"

The hologram winks out.

"Mr. Riley will provide the people of California with entertainment to work off his debt to society."

The crowd applauds.

"You mean I'll be forced to kill people like them so they won't lynch corrupt swine like you."

"Bailiffs!" The judge turns red. "Take the prisoner away and hook him into the interface."

More cheers. The bailiffs grab my shackled arms and drag me toward the tunnel. I catch my mother and sister up in the stands. No one else in the back row has black hair and pale skin like me. They're hugging each other and weeping.

"Don't sweat it, Donny boy." My lawyer shoots a finger gun at me. "We'll catch an appeal. Just don't die in the first week, 'kay?"

The steel doors slam shut behind me. It's silent in here. Empty and cold. The bailiffs guide me down a white-tiled hallway. They stuff me into an elevator tube and punch the outside button. My stomach drops as the tube falls. I slam to a halt, and the doors whisk open.

It looks like a cavern. Jumpsuited guards grab my arms and lead me toward the edge of a massive pit. Its honeycomb walls disappear into the abyss. I can see no bottom, but voices echo far below.

The guards stop at an open black container. Its hexagonal length would slide right into one of those honeycomb holes. We're close enough to the pit's edge that I can see hundreds, maybe thousands of other containers lying inside those holes.

"Wait, you're stuffing me in that coffin thing? And shoving me into that wall with all those other people?"

"This is your cell, kid," a balding guard says. "A short ride into the digital world."

Two women in white coats approach us from the side.

"Everything ready?" the same guard asks a lab-coat lady with horn-rimmed glasses. She's middle aged, olive skinned, and smoking hot.

"Yes. Strip the inmate and place him in the immersion chamber. Kaley?"

Her lanky assistant steps forward.

"Prep the feeding tube, dock the Neurohelm, and insert the stimulation needles into the spinal cord."

Kaley pulls out a metal bucket covered with pulsating green lights and a tray of clear tubes tipped in inch-long spikes.

Panic hits. "You can't do this. You can't just go along with it."

Everyone ignores me.

"You're sentencing people to death. Don't you get that? First, you stuff us in these coffins; then we're killed for sport. You're just as guilty as anybody buried down here. I demand a retrial!"

A guard kicks the backs of my knees. I drop to the floor. MILFina stabs a syringe in my neck, and I go limp.

Rough hands lift me into the coffin. I plunge into absolute darkness.

CHAPTER 2

FINAL LOGIN

The whole world is black. In my panic, I wonder if someone screwed up the immersion software. *Is this gonna be my sentence, just endless silence in a hole?*

A dialogue box opens before my eyes with a flashing cursor.

Enter username.

"I got your username right here."

MyJudgeWasAHog
Not valid. Usernames may not insult People's Republic of California party members.
ScrewYou
Not valid. Usernames may not display aggression toward the viewing audience.

"Seriously? Let a guy express himself a little." I think it over. A new world. A new life. A chance to screw everything up again.

BrokenChains
Username accepted. Welcome to *God's Staircase*, BrokenChains.

The black explodes into white and blurs to blue. A harsh wind peels back my eyelids. I'm free falling from the stratosphere with a rugged landscape splayed beneath me. The wind tears at my homespun clothes. I try to shout, "What, not even a parachute?" But my lips are flapping so hard it sounds more like "Hrflmrglgle?"

"You've got to me kidding me. Are you gonna kill me before I even get a chance? Hey, someone help me!"

A black window shimmers to life in front of me. It matches my speed as I plummet toward the mountain range below. Rachel Justice appears against a Victorian street corner backdrop in all her bodacious bikini glory.

"Welcome, BrokenChains, to *God's Staircase*. You're in for the steampunk ride of a lifetime."

"Hey, help me! Someone set the entry point wrong, and I'm gonna die." I hope her software can interpret the garbled words pouring from my wind-flapped lips.

"Silly inmate." Rachel titters. "You won't get off that easy. You'll have time to regret your mistakes as you fight your way up God's Staircase. Just relax and enjoy your opening cutscene."

A red light blinks in my top-left field of vision. **Now streaming** flashes across my view of the snowcapped range below.

"Remember," Rachel says as we fall, "the bigger the action, the more viewers we give your stream."

"What kind of action?"

Rachel points down at the largest mountain. I'm pretty sure nothing that tall exists on Earth, but I'm no mountainologist. White marble platforms stack up the ultramountain's side. It really does look like a staircase.

"Your objective is simple, BrokenChains. Clear all fifty steps on God's Staircase, and everyone on your server will be freed."

"We get to go home?"

"That's right." Rachel beams. Her digital boobs give a dramatic bounce.

"So I'll land safely?"

Rachel presses a finger to the corner of her mouth. Her boobs wobble again as she ponders. "I think so. They probably worked out the crash issue by now."

"You said I wasn't gonna die, you digital bimbo!"

"I said you'd have time to regret your mistakes. New players' five-minute average lifespan should be enough." Rachel scrunches her nose and sticks out her tongue. She'd be adorable if she wasn't handing down my death sentence.

"Before I forget," Rachel adds, "you're facing the new Attendant program. He's pretty feisty. Got all handsy on our date." Another mindless titter.

Who programmed this babe?

"Keep your eyes peeled for his secret hands behind the scenes because when the viewers at home get bored, the Attendant is authorized to ramp up the action."

"Mob us to death, you mean?"

"The Attendant's there to keep the action flowing, not slaughter players with overwhelming force." A worried frown creases her face but flips into a smile. "I think they fixed that bug, too."

"You *think*?"

Rachel shoots a flirty glance past me like she's making eye contact with someone over my shoulder. Her tits wiggle in perfect time with her eyebrows. "Stay tuned, viewers. We've got plenty of exciting new features in store, including the death arena where inmates compete for fabulous prizes!"

"All the cyborg ponies in the PRC couldn't drag me into that arena."

"You say that now." Rachel wags her finger at me. "Wait till you get the hang of the game."

"In the next five minutes?"

"That's just the average. This game's only been open a week, so you shouldn't be too far behind the other degenerates."

"What did you call me?"

"You've been staring at my breasts this whole time, BrokenChains. I call 'em like I see 'em. Happy landing!"

"Are you really an AI?"

Rachel winks. Just one boob jiggles. Her window screenwipes, leaving me to free fall at terminal velocity toward the pearly stairs' lowest step. It's grown from a white domino to a miles-wide ledge with an urban sprawl across its bottom half.

I scream as I rocket toward a big square teeming with people in Victorian clothes. The cobblestones rush up, and my whole body clenches for impact.

Invisible forces arrest my fall. I float the last few feet, screaming like a schoolgirl with my eyes puckered shut. When my feet touch the cobblestones, I collapse like a bag of jelly and kiss the salty ground.

Clucking laughter draws my eyes to five women giggling behind their hands. Some dude with a huge beard guffaws so hard he collapses next to the cluster of hens. I ignore the rest of the laughing mob, climb to my feet, and come face-to-face with two thugs. One is stocky with a grimy face. The other's the size and shape of a car door. Both wear copper hoods.

"Getting pinched for battery doesn't make you batteries, guys."

"Shut it," the burly one on the right barks. Glowing letters above his head read **LootThatBooty**. "Open your trade window, and hand over your starting goods."

I cup my ear. "What's that? Sorry . . . I don't take orders from anyone who looks like the server messed up and swapped his butt with his face."

Booty moves in till the cutlass hilts jutting from our wide belts clack together. "Hand it over. Now. Or you're dead."

"Whoa, your breath proves my hunch." I shove him two paces back with no lag, like my digital arm is my real arm. His sackcloth shirt scratches my palm.

The whole game feels real—deadly real.

Booty's short companion rushes me and waves a crude knife under my nose. Green letters reading **FearTheStumpo** float in front of my eyes. "Last chance, funnyman."

I raise my hands. "OK, gimme a sec. How do I—?"

"Like this." Booty raises his right hand diagonally with his first two fingers extended and swipes up.

I repeat his gesture, and a menu pops open. A candy store of text and buttons fills my screen, but I quickly locate my inventory. Several empty boxes surround a silhouette of my body. But **Rough Shirt, Rough Pants, Rough Boots, Rough Belt, Rough Gloves, Iron Cutlass,** and **Oaken Shield** are equipped in their corresponding slots. All have single-digit stats.

"I hate to tell you, boys, but my starting gear sucks."

Stumpo takes a step back but keeps me at knifepoint. "Just unequip it and open a trade window. Give us your starting cash, too."

"Cash?" A little bag sits in my inventory's bottom-right corner next to a silver coin and the number twenty.

"Cash." Booty snaps his fingers impatiently. "I'm gonna count to three."

"Don't strain your math skills," I deadpan.

Booty's smile doesn't touch his dull eyes. "Clothes, too."

I close my window with a hard slide to the right. Stumpo and Booty curse as I pull the Iron Cutlass from my belt and yank the round oaken shield off my back. Its solid weight settles comfortably on my left arm. "I drop my pants for no man. You morons want my clothes, you're gonna have to take 'em."

Stumpo lunges for my guts with his knife flashing. I slam my shield down. His blade scrapes wood, and he snarls. The shield hides his knife hand from my view.

Booty draws his sword and throws himself at my right side with a war cry. I parry his cutlass with my own. The blow vibrates up my arm, and I back away to give myself space to breathe.

Stumpo creeps to my left. I strain to see his knife hand, but Booty slashes again. I duck under his whirring blade and stab at his stomach. He bounds back, and his next swing clobbers me in the side of the head.

I've seen public safety counselors waste more than one food rioter the same way—and with batons, not swords. Instead of blood spraying from my cloven skull, red pixels explode out of my intact head. A migraine-like pulse washes over me.

I'm still reeling when Stumpo reaches past my shield and sticks my left side. A stomach cramp twists my gut. The green health bar in the top left corner of my vision turns one-third yellow, and the pain fades.

"That's it?" I bark a laugh. "That's what getting hurt here feels like? Back home we call that cuddling. Let's try this again, gutter rats."

I throw myself at Stumpo. His little knife flashes again, but I slam his stained teeth with my shield. A health bar appears below his floating name text and drops by 10 percent. I drive my cutlass into Stumpo's substantial gut. His health bar drops to half. The little punk screams like a stuck pig as red pixels slither from his wound.

"Pussy," I taunt him.

Booty drives his blade into my exposed back. Pain erupts between my shoulder blades as my health bar drops to half. I rip my sword through Stumpo's side, step off Booty's cutlass, and kick Stumpo in his barrel chest. Townsfolk scatter as the little squealer goes rolling across the cobbles.

A clutch of female inmates in shabby dresses trade coins. One scrawny blonde licks her lips at me.

I whirl to meet Booty's next thrust. His blade bounces off my shield, and I stab low from behind cover. He squawks like an exotic bird as my cutlass pierces his junk. My follow-up shield bash crunches into his face and spills him on his butt. A streak of red pixels briefly gives him a joker's smile as my blade splits his head. With a scream, he drops his sword to clutch his face. His health bar hovers at 20 percent.

Please," Booty gasps, "no more!"

I loom over the copper-cowled thugs with a menacing grin. "You come at the king, you best not miss."

A flurry of text erupts across my vision.

One-handed Swords skill increased to 2.
Shields skill increased to 2.
Defense skill increased to 2.
Brawling skill increased to 2.
Intimidate skill increased to 2.

"Looks like you morons just made me stronger. Want another beatdown?"

Booty and Stumpo share a dismayed look and shake their heads.

I wave my cutlass between them. "Then open your trade windows. All's fair in love and prison muggings."

Before any goods change hands, clattering footsteps draw my attention across the square. Ten more goons in copper hoods burst through the audience with weapons in hand. They take one look at the two Hoods cowering at my feet and surround me like a wolf pack.

Stumpo gets up and rushes out of the ring with a yelp. Booty scoots backward and cries, "Boss, this guy's nuts!"

"Quit bitching." A muscly ponytailed dude in black leather armor stalks toward me, clutching a clockwork mace in both hands. **ChocolateReaper** hangs over his copper-hooded head. "You let a noob take you down, Booty? I'm gonna splatter this guy, and then I'm gonna give you your performance review."

"He's a beast, Reap! I never seen a guy use a shield like that."

Reaper and the nine other Hoods encircling me raise the hairs on my neck, but being scared pisses me off. I nod to Booty and Stumpo. "These your boys? I found them roughing up newcomers. Piss-poor inmate orientation."

"Crossing the Copper Hoods fast-tracks you from orientation to retirement." Reaper smirks. "See you in hell, smart guy."

I spit on the cobblestones. "Big tough guys, dogpiling a newbie with starting gear and half health. What do you say we make this interesting and call it a duel?"

"Nah." Reaper laughs. "We're gonna cut you till you shatter."

"'Shatter' sounds bad."

"It is. Means you die."

The ten Hoods lunge at me. One thug on my left spills across the pavement when someone from outside the kill circle punts him. The newcomer leaps in front of me to face Reaper. His heavy leather boots, padded frock coat, and fancy top hat signal his higher place on the curve.

"You want to murder a noob, you must go through me." My savior's got an orator's voice. The green text over his head reads **PerfectBlade**. He slides two sabers from his belt and strikes a smooth combat stance.

ChocolateReaper rushes him with a snarl and a heavy swing from his clockwork mace. PerfectBlade ducks under the blow and scissors his sabers across Reaper's stomach. Red pixels burst from the overlapping wounds, and his health drops from full to 10 percent.

The black-clad thug falls to one knee with a groan. He clutches his stomach, glaring up at the warrior who stands over him with both sabers ready to strike.

"Withdraw," PerfectBlade orders the Copper Hoods.

All twelve Hoods turn tail and skulk from the town square, leaving PerfectBlade and me alone with the murmuring audience. Sacks of coins change hands as the winners laugh and the losers grumble. My savior slides his blades back into his belt.

"Thanks for the save," I tell him.

He turns to me with an easy smile on his youthful superhero face and extends a hand. "Folks call me Perfect. Because I am."

"No argument here." I grab his offered hand in the arm wrestler's shake banned by the PRC. "Call me Chains."

"You're lucky I happened by." His mouth twists in a disgusted grimace. "Too many predators sniffing around."

"Not to sound ungrateful, but why'd you stick your neck out?"

"We're all stuck in this death game together. Someone's got to keep the peace. How new are you?"

"About five minutes now."

Perfect's pretty-boy smile returns. "You beat the average. Let me show you the ropes."

"I'm not much of a socialite, but I'll tag along for a while."

"A good crew is a necessity here, Chains. Predators hunt the weak and the lonely."

"What kind of batshit prison doesn't have guards?"

Perfect scoffs. "Welcome to Geartown."

CHAPTER 3

A BARGAIN IS STRUCK

We hustle through the narrow, winding streets. Victorian buildings loom over us. Turning gears and hissing pipes poke from every nook and cranny.

"This place looks like a demented engineer's wet dream," I say.

Perfect throws me an amused glance over his shoulder. "The first two death games' generic fantasy setting got old fast, so the PRC held a referendum to pick this game's theme. Now we get to live and die in a steampunk prison."

"Steampunk got the most votes?"

"No. The PRC said it got the most votes." Perfect signals a halt atop a bridge arcing over the road below. "This is the Vendors' Quarter." He sweeps his gloved hand over a maze of hissing, clicking city blocks. Steel girders sparkle in the sunlight as clockwork sparrows flit under the wide eaves of patchwork sheet-metal rooftops.

"It's weird knowing that's not the real sun," I think aloud.

"The game's night-day cycle follows the outside world, so your circadian rhythm won't have to adjust. Are you a normal sleeper or a night owl?"

"I get up pretty early. Been working two jobs to feed my family since I was twelve. But I guess that's everyone in the PRC."

"So I hear. The Vendors' Quarter has everything a budding warrior could need. Especially potions—you'll need to stock up on those since there's no magic here. Healing potions will be your new addiction. Your starting gear won't last you past level five. You'll need to save up enough cash for upgrades or focus on quests with gear rewards."

"How do I get money? Besides robbing people in the town square, I mean."

"Loot drops. Kill a monster, chances are it dumps an item in a little brown sack. Scoop that up and sell it in town for profit. Later on you can pick up a side job and use the drops for crafting. Or you take a job gathering, mining, or fishing and sell those resources."

"Great, I get to work part time as I serve my prison sentence."

Perfect laughs. "Don't knock it. A million platinum buys you an extra life."

I almost miss a step. "Extra life? As in, they don't microwave my brain if I die in the game?"

"So the vendor data says. It's an item called Phoenix Tears. A smoking-hot princess NPC up in the castle sells the premium items."

"Now I've got something to shoot for." I survey the clacking, steamy streets below. "First things first. Let's buy me some better gear."

"Your starting coin won't go far in the arms shops. I recommend saving it for an inn. You don't want to be broke and homeless in this game."

"Why? Nights get cold?"

Perfect's eyes narrow. "Hearts get colder. Player killers bag half their victims' wealth."

"That why those thugs jumped me?"

"The Copper Hoods prefer to mug people for the full amount, but as my father says, 'Desperation breeds haste and waste.' There are worse predators than Reaper's crew in Geartown, Chains. Stay off the streets after dark."

"So I've got to pay rent on an apartment, too. Leave it to bureaucrats to build a game that keeps players paying bills."

"Save up enough, and you can buy your own guild house at level eighty."

"I'll think about it."

"Don't think too long. Lone wolves get picked off fast. It's only been a week, and I've seen more murders here than on the outside. A wall stands on the city's south edge at the bottom of this step. The name of every player who dies gets inscribed on that monument, along with the cause of death. Don't let me see you on there, OK, Chains?"

His tone sobers me up like a bucket of ice water. "They really threw hardened murderers in here with the low-level offenders?"

"Sure did. And no consequences for killing anyone in the game. Constitutional rights of every inmate are suspended. We're not people again until our sentence is served."

"No one tries to stop the carnage?"

Perfect laughs. "They're all criminals, Chains. I had to commit a crime to get in here. So did you. Or are you innocent like everybody claims to be?"

"No." I break eye contact and look out over the city. "I'm guilty as hell."

Perfect props his back against the stone railing beside me. "This world's dark, but it's gonna get darker the higher we push up the mountain. This server's already close to max capacity. All ten thousand of us need to work together to get out, but trust is a rare commodity."

I remember Reaper's boys trying to roll me in broad daylight with a crowd of miserable bastards cheering them on. My hands ball into fists. "I've seen my share of bloodletting, but nothing like this."

Perfect punches my shoulder. "You're already thinking of ways to make this place better; am I right?"

"With no laws, vigilantism sounds tempting."

"Gonna need some levels before you can stop the villains, hero. Speaking of which, let's head out of town. I'll give you some pointers on combat."

I meet his questing eye. "What's in it for you, Perfect? Why are you helping me?"

His surprised look gives way to laughter. "A little paranoia will keep you alive. But don't worry about me, Chains. I honestly want strong men at my side to help clear the game. I want to get everyone out of here, and the best way is to build the best army. I saw how you handled those thugs. Your raw skill got my attention. I'll help you refine it, and in return, you give serious thought to joining my team. Deal?"

My father's disappointed face pops into my head. The thought of seeing that raw look of betrayal on someone else burns the pit of my stomach, but I dredge up my courage and nod. "Deal, bro. I'll do whatever it takes to get home to my family. Teach me to survive this game."

"Done." Perfect pushes off the stone railing. "Let's head out to the forest and kill some cyborgs."

CHAPTER 4

KILLING LIKE CLOCKWORK

The crowds get thicker as we approach Geartown's northern clockwork wall. I follow Perfect on a winding course through knots of frock-coated men who meet our looks with sneers. They're chatting up a pack of women whose corsets hike their tits up to their powdered chins.

Everyone's armed to the teeth—even the girls wearing more brass than clothing.

A whiff of spicy grilled meat rises above the stink of smoke, machine oil, and musky perfume. "Something smells good," I shout to Perfect over the buzz of the crowd.

Perfect nods. "Plenty of places to eat. The game devs at Cryoblend emulated most flavors well enough. The burritos at Ugly Johnny's are to die for. You can try them when we get back."

We stride through an arch in the wall. An iron portcullis hangs twenty feet overhead. The ramparts are at least ten feet thick, and the shade cools my skin. On the other side, bright sunlight strikes my face. A worn dirt path runs from the city gate to the horizon through rolling grasslands.

"Your health is back to full, right?"

I check the upper left corner of my vision, and my health bar enlarges. It's solid green. "Yeah, I've healed up to max."

"Spending time in the city does that. It's the one way to heal apart from items like potions. If you're about to die, head back to town. Just make sure no one stabs you while you're here." Perfect pats me on the back, but a chill runs down my spine.

"Hey, gate guard," Perfect calls to a guy in heavy armor standing beside the arch. "Any quests for us today?"

The sentry tips his huge hunting spear to us. "Good day, travelers. Her Majesty's army could use your assistance clearing a nest of cyborg goblins from the Whispering Wood."

Perfect shoots him a thumbs-up. "That's what we're looking for. Give us the details."

"Goblins have been raiding our settlements all over the area." The guard's eyes narrow in anger. "Killed a few soldiers, too. Wipe 'em out, and choose a randomly generated reward."

A little blip of light appears and expands to a text window. The lengthy backstory ends with a call to help Her Majesty's army protect the citizens of God's Staircase.

"I ain't here to play pretend." I jab the **Accept Quest** button at the bottom of the window. Text appears to my right and enlarges when I focus on it.

Clearing the Wood
Slay goblins—0/20

"Simple enough."

"Good hunting, travelers." The guard turns back to his vigil. Perfect and I stride down the wide dirt road leading north.

I glance back at the guard once we're out of earshot. "Easy gig for a prisoner. How'd he get a guard posting?"

"He's not an inmate. He's an NPC run by the game's AI."

"Pretty good facial expressions and verbal delivery for a computer program."

"Yeah, PRC spared no expense building their death game. Gotta look great for the viewers at home."

"How do you tell the real people from the NPCs?"

Perfect chuckles. "It can be tough, but if you start talking about something beyond their understanding, like the game mechanics, NPCs get this hazy look and say, 'I'm sorry, traveler. I didn't understand that.'"

"That's messed up."

"It's like talking to a normal-looking person who turns out to be in a cult. Most people play along and only talk to NPCs when they have to."

"When do they have to?"

"NPCs run a lot of shops, work as gate guards, and hand out quests. There's even a smoking-hot waitress at Ugly Johnny's who'll give you a strip tease in the kitchen if you tip well enough."

I shake my head. "I'll skip the AI sex workers and focus on staying alive."

The dirt path splits to the west, north, and east. Perfect and I turn right to head east. A heat haze wavers on the far horizon. Battles between adventuring parties and bands of monsters dot the rolling grasslands. We pass a group of teenage girls in brightly colored dresses. Their squeals pierce my ears as they swing at a little slime that's bouncing around with a big smile.

Perfect claps my shoulder. "You itching to try your sword on something more lucrative than thugs?"

"You read my mind."

"Let's get some practice before we head into the quest zone." He points to our left. "Try taking on that clockwork hawk."

My eyes follow his finger to a clockwork bird half as big as me. Its red eyes flash as it swoops over the rippling grass. When it reaches the edge of its territory, it wheels back in the opposite direction.

"Let's party up so we share experience." Perfect raises his hand, swipes open his window, and taps at hidden menus like a mime pretending to type.

A little window pops up. **PerfectBlade has invited you to join a party.** I click the **Accept** button, then click **Accept** again on a window that says **PerfectBlade has sent a friend request.**

Perfect's dashing portrait and green health bar appear along the left edge of my vision. He's already level 10.

"This way we can keep track of each other even if we split up. We'll share all our kills, too. The game awards loot randomly to party members, but we can divvy those up later."

"Trust doesn't come easy to me, Perfect, but I'll give you a shot."

"Thanks. First up, dodging and blocking practice. That hawk will swoop straight at you to start. Get the timing wrong, and you take a nasty hit. Think you can handle it?"

"I got this." I draw my cutlass and shield as I stride down from the dirt path and into the knee-high grass. The hawk's blood-red eyes lock onto me. It looses a tinny screech and dives at me. Its razor beak slices a line of crimson pixels across my chest. My pecs burn.

"Damn!" I check my health bar. Luckily, it's only down 10 percent.

"Don't take this guy lightly, Chains," Perfect calls from the sidelines. "I'll step in before he kills you, but it'll hurt."

The hawk swivels around and darts at me again. I raise my shield, and the brass raptor slams into it. The surprisingly strong impact sends me backpedaling three paces.

Despite not flapping its wings, the hawk wobbles in midair. It retreats before I can recover and spreads its wings for another charge. I brace my feet wide and angle my shield twenty degrees. At the moment of impact, I thrust the oak slab forward and left like I'm pushing through a door. The clockwork hawk bounces off in a spray of tiny gears as a light tremor shoots up my arm.

The hawk reels back. I step in and slash with my cutlass. A pixelated gash rips across the bird's torso. The red health bar that appears above its head drains by a quarter.

Screaming, the hawk flaps away. It spins to charge me again, and I repeat the shield-bash-to-cutlass-slash maneuver. Before it can retreat, I add a second hit and take its health down to a quarter.

Perfect lifts his coattails and takes a seat on the hill sloping down from the road. "That bash at the moment of impact seems to increase the temporary Stagger effect."

"Doesn't tear my arm off or send me flying when I take the hit, either."

"How's the cutlass feel?"

"Heavy. It's balanced OK, but it's nothing special."

"The better your gear, the more comfortable it feels. Remember that when you pick up swords made by player vendors. Whoops, here he comes again."

The hawk dives at me with a screech. Instead of angling my shield to the side, I bash the bird into the ground. It bounces in the grass and sits there swaying as stars circle its head.

"Nice work," says Perfect. "That's the Stunned effect. You've got five uninterrupted seconds to beat on him."

I slash the hawk's head. A **Critical Hit** alert flashes above the monster's health bar as it drops to zero. An inner glow shatters its body into a million red shards that rain down on the grass.

Perfect gives me a thumbs-up. "Got your first kill. Satisfying, right?"

"Damn straight," I say as notifications flash across my vision.

One-handed Swords skill increased to 4.
Shields skill increased to 4.
Defense skill increased to 4.
20 XP gained.

"The spoils of battle," says Perfect.

"Do monsters always explode into glass?"

"Everything that dies. Monsters leave red glass; players leave green. No one's seen an NPC's death color yet. The devs made them tough to kill."

I consider the shards scattered around my feet. "Imagine if that's all you had left of someone important to you."

Perfect laughs. "Don't be so morbid. The glass vanishes after a minute. We've got a tower to clear and a server to liberate. Feel like you've got the hang of combat?"

I roll my shoulders. "Glassing monsters ain't as satisfying as pounding on thugs, but . . ."

"Let's try some teamwork." Perfect rises to his feet, dusts off his black coat, and heads toward another hawk circling a few dozen feet away. "You take his charge, then we both slash him."

I rush ahead of Perfect with my shield up. The hawk pivots toward me with a scream and charges. I bash the metal bird aside, and it wobbles in midair with stars around his head.

Perfect rushes up and scissors his gleaming sabers through the hawk's head as I slash its torso with my flimsy iron blade. Its health bar drops to zero, and its clockwork body bursts into a shower of red glass, leaving behind a little brown sack tied with a string.

My name hovers just above the bag in tiny white letters. Skill notifications flash across my vision, telling me I've become even more badass. I pick up the nearly weightless bag. "This the loot you told me about?"

"That's it," says Perfect. "I can't pick it up because it's tagged for you. Nicely done."

"Thanks. What do I do with this?"

"Just picture yourself putting the bag in your pocket as you crush it in your fist."

I curl my fingers around the bag. It disappears in a sparkle of white light, and a soft chime sounds.

"It just went into your inventory," Perfect says.

Checking the specified window shows me a toothed wheel labeled **Iron Gear**. "Righteous."

"Make sure you pick up all the loot bags tagged with your name."

"Gotta save up for one of those burritos, right? What's next?"

"If you've got the hang of basic combat, let's head into the Whispering Wood and take out those twenty goblins."

We sheathe our weapons and march back to the road.

"You haven't done this quest yet?" I ask as we continue down the trail.

"I have, but it's a repeatable quest. Some folks make their living farming one quest per day or a handful of noncombat fetch quests. Few players repeat this goblin quest since it's more dangerous than most, but the rewards are good."

"What about players who ain't hardcore gladiators like us?"

Perfect waves halfheartedly. "A lot of the female players gather herbs outside town. They either post one of their own as a guard or put a paid male player on monster watch. Just about anyone can survive in here as long as they're willing to live on the bottom rung."

"And people leave them alone?"

"This is a prison, Chains. We've got no shortage of predators. The Copper Hoods are the most notorious, but plenty others try to press the female players into sex work. It's as lucrative here as on the outside. A couple of the gangs run camgirl channels in here and take donations from viewers."

I raise an eyebrow. "What good does real-world cash do them in here?"

"You can exchange real money for game currency. It's big business. The girls you see gathering herbs are the ones who stay out of the smut trade—if they pay their bodyguards enough"

"Lovely." My fists clench.

"Does the reality of prison life bother you?"

"Doesn't it bother you, Perfect?"

"That's why I'm gathering the manpower to stop the chaos. But life on the outside's not much better. Last year the PRC lowered the minimum sex worker age to fourteen."

"I remember. The news said it'd reduce teen depression and suicide. Now girls under eighteen are dancing in strip clubs. I busted my ass to keep my sister out of places like that."

"No sense weeping over man's inhumanity to man. What we can do is get enough power to make them be better."

"We can protect them, too."

"You'll never raise your level guarding herb-pickers. Someone stronger just comes along, kills you, and takes them anyway."

My teeth grind together. "There's gotta be a better way."

"If you find it, let me know."

We walk in silence to the edge of a shady forest. The path fades from sight a few yards into the trees.

"Here's where the game really starts," says Perfect. "Try not to die."

CHAPTER 5

AN OFFER REFUSED

Perfect leads me into the murky woods with his sabers drawn. The soothing winds and birdsong of the plains give way to eerily rustling leaves and the occasional hooting of unseen owls. Every breath tastes like vegetables rotting in wet earth.

I pull my cutlass and shield. "Shouldn't I be up front?"

"Goblins patrol pretty far from their spawn points." Perfect scans the head-high brush that flanks the path. "At your level, you wouldn't survive an ambush."

I grip my weapons tight and try to peer ahead, but the gloom limits visibility to ten feet. "Cryoblend did a great job making this place believable."

"Yeah, you could almost forget the real world. Hey, you hear that?"

I strain my hearing and get a notification that my Perception skill has increased. Guttural snarling drifts through the trees. "Sounds like roided-out raccoons."

"Goblin speech," Perfect whispers. "Keep quiet from here." He crouches low and stalks through the trees. I follow close behind.

Perfect parts the brush to reveal a wide clearing splashed with dancing firelight. Four warty green runts sit around a crude camp, growling in their hideous tongue. Clockwork pincers and pneumatic peg legs jut from their mismatched pirate outfits.

"I'll take the two on the right," Perfect whispers in my ear. "Think you can handle the other two?"

The leftmost goblin has a glowing red eye and a clockwork leg that whirrs as he shifts position. His buddy's right arm ends in a vicious brass hook. Like the others, they've got machetes stuffed in their belts.

"They meaner than the two thugs I roughed up in town?" I ask, using my indoor voice.

Perfect nods. "Yes, but they're more predictable."

"No problem. This feels wrong, though. They're sitting there babbling like old friends. That guy just handed his buddy a wineskin. We're really gonna run in there and kill them?"

"They're programs, Chains. They exist for us to kill them. If we don't, they'll kill us."

"Point taken." I draw a deep breath. "Let's do it."

"Make it fast. First strike often determines the winner." Perfect rushes into the clearing. He slices off the rightmost goblin's head before the little creature can stand up.

I charge the goblin with the hook. He's already rising as I swing my cutlass. The blow catches him across his frilly-shirted torso. He rolls back into the dirt, but his health bar only falls 20 percent.

My second goblin's ruffled collar makes him look like a frilled lizard. His machete flashes in his mechanical hand. I block with my shield, throw his blade wide, and slash at his gut. The goblin dodges. His machete chops into my sword arm with a wave of pain. I almost drop my saber as my health bar slides from 90 to 75 percent.

"I'm already down a quarter of my health. These guys are brutal!"

Perfect keeps his eye on the goblin he's dueling across the camp. "Then stop complaining and kill them!"

I rush the ruffled goblin, slam my shield into his torso, and hurl him to the ground. He writhes in the dirt. I pounce on him and stab his little paunch gut. His agonized howls turn my stomach, but I keep stabbing. His health bar plummets to 30 percent.

A line of pain burns across my back, and I lose another third of my health. I force down a scream and jump to my feet. The hook goblin stands behind me, brandishing his machete. Our blades clash without scoring any hits. I shield bash him, inflicting the Stagger effect, and follow up by slamming the oaken edge into his face. He squawks as stars ring his wobbling head. I fly into a frenzy and cut him until he bursts into red fragments.

The ruffled goblin at my back stands up and shrieks a battle cry. I spin to take his strike on my shield, but he angles to my other side. His machete arcs toward my face. I'm about to die.

My father's face passes before my eyes. He shakes his head in disgust.

Perfect's twin blades quarter the frilled goblin's head. The beast explodes in a shower of glass that pelts me like red hail.

"Looks like you owe me another one." Perfect's voice matches his smirk.

Text fills my vision. Still in a daze at having narrowly survived, I let my eyes drift across the words.

You reached Level 2!
Now able to equip gear requiring level 2 and below.
Health and Stamina increased.
Skill rank caps increased to 20.
One-handed Swords skill increased to 12.
Shields skill increased to 14.
Defense skill increased to 11.
Stealth increased to 6.
500 XP gained.

My health bar refills to maximum, which is a small amount higher than before. "Gaining a level takes the edge off looking death in the eye."

"Yeah," says Perfect, "leveling up can be— Look out!"

I spin around and catch an arrow in the guts. Red pixels fountain from my torso as agony sears through my middle. My new health bar drops by 30 percent. Worse, it turns purple and keeps draining.

"Poison." Perfect shoulders me aside and hurls a knife at a goblin archer lurking in the bushes. The blade sinks into the goblin's forehead.

He falls back and shatters. Four more goblins leap from the bushes with machetes waving.

"How do I stop the poison?"

"Antidote," says Perfect. "I've got one, but we need to kill these guys first." He parries the first machete and returns a vicious slash to the wielder's green face. His follow-up strike skewers the goblin through the heart and empties its health bar. Perfect rushes through the shower of red glass to attack his next target.

Fighting back nausea, I seize the feathered shaft sprouting from my gut and rip it out. The burning disappears, but the sick feeling remains, and my health continues to drain at an alarming rate.

"I can't die here." The crash of battle drowns out my whisper. "Mom and Sis need me."

A goblin charges me with his machete raised. I block his strike with my blade and shield bash him off his piston feet. I pin his torso to the ground on my cutlass and batter his face with my shield until he explodes in a shower of red glass.

More red flecks pepper me as Perfect glasses the third goblin. The fourth and final beast charges him from behind. I hurl myself between them, and my shield takes the machete blow. Perfect thrusts one blade through the goblin's meat eye and the other through its robot eye. A pulse of light blows it into scarlet shards that rattle against my shield.

I collapse to one knee in exhaustion. My purple health dwindles to 40 percent. "Got that antidote?"

Perfect opens his invisible menu and taps the air a few times. A glass vial of sparkling green fluid appears in his hand. He tosses it to me. "Chug this."

I pop the little stopper and gulp down the contents. It tastes like charcoal sweetened with maraschino cherry. The vial bursts into tiny white pixels. My health bar changes from purple to red and stabilizes.

"I'm at 35 percent left."

"Now try this." Perfect manifests another vial, this one full of glowing red fluid. It tastes like sweet peaches. My health bar immediately refills to maximum, and I breathe a sigh of relief as notifications flood my vision.

You reached Level 3!
Now able to equip gear requiring level 3 and below.
Health and Stamina increased.
Skill rank caps increased to 30.
One-handed Swords skill increased to 17.
Shields skill increased to 19.
Defense skill increased to 19.
625 XP gained.

"Looks like I didn't need the health potion after all. But thanks, bro." I stand up on shaky legs. "How can I be this tired? This isn't even my real body."

"Cryoblend hijacks the signals from your body so your brain thinks the digital version is real. You start off with your real-world endurance levels and grow from there."

"Glad I spent all those mornings working out." The red shards have all disappeared and left behind a cluster of bags, so I scoop up the two with my name on them and crush them into my inventory.

"You good to keep going, or did that arrow scare you off?"

"Can't stop now, right? I'll never get home if an arrow to the guts scares me off."

"Cool. That's nine goblins down, eleven to go. We can even kill a few extra to round out your experience gain. What level are you now?"

"Just hit three."

"Outstanding. Let's get you to five before we head back."

• • • •

Perfect and I kill goblins like we're out to extinctify their whole species. He shows me how to spot them through the brush, how to move silently to avoid detection, and which body parts to target for critical hits. By the time we finish, I've hit level 6 and killed so many goblins I see them less as ugly humans and more as rabid animals or lawyers.

As we stride from the forest, sunlight smacks me in the face. I squint and see the sky tinged orange. "Sunset already?"

"Time flies when you're killing monsters, huh? Besides, you logged in late in the afternoon."

"'Logged in,' is a nice way of saying I got stuffed in a coffin and sealed into a wall. Wonder what's happening to my body right now."

"Just pretend a ravishing nurse is taking care of you. Come on, we need to get back before dark."

We jog down the dirt road back to Geartown. Perfect slides open his menu and taps a few invisible buttons. "A deal's a deal. Here's your share of the swag."

I open my inventory. "An iron gear and fifteen goblin teeth. If I ask the gangs nice, you think they'd let me strip for real cash?"

Perfect raises a cautioning finger. "Not so fast. Mechanical enemies give great crafting drops. Best way to upgrade your gear. Monster enemies mostly drop sellable items, though a few will give hides you can turn into leather."

"Slow down, Buffalo Bill. What's the street value of this stuff?"

"The marketplace is super hit or miss. Make sure you check before dumping your items at a vendor, just in case you get something rare. Most people don't bother with that unless they're trying to level up the Merchant skill."

"I'm not really the outdoor type," I confess, "but going into business sounds interesting."

We're standing at the front gates before the sun hits the horizon. The same guard who sent us to the forest eyes us as we approach.

"Welcome back, travelers. Did you splatter those goblins for us?"

Perfect flashes him a grin. "It was pure genocide."

"Excellent. Feel free to take one of the following rewards." The guard holds out his empty hand like he's offering me something. A window pops up in front of me with some more splash text about serving Her Majesty. I click through to the reward items. A cluster of health potions draws my eye since I've got none of my own, but the upgraded shield seems like a better choice. I tap that one and confirm the selection. A soft chime and a line of text let me know the **Goblin Tooth Shield** has been deposited to my inventory.

"Not sure I want to know what that looks like . . ." Despite my misgivings, I tap the **Inspect** button.

Goblin Tooth Shield
Armor rating 24 (Currently equipped shield 6.)
Adds piercing damage to shield bash attacks.

I open my inventory and drag the reward item into my shield slot. The oaken shield ripples with light and changes to a circle of wood with lacquered yellow teeth embedded in the front.

"Good choice," Perfect says. "Most of your gear is outdated now. You should head to an armorsmith for some upgrades. Your Defense skill gives you protection when unarmored, but unless you're going for an agile build like archer or scoundrel, armor is the way to go."

"Sounds good." I stow the shield on my back and hold out my hand. "Thanks for your time today. And for saving my ass."

Perfect grasps my hand. "Just keeping my end of the bargain. I hope you'll keep yours."

"Mine?"

"Your promise to consider my offer. Once I hit level eighty, I'm opening a guild. Already got a fancy name: Knights of the Golden Dawn. We could use a fighter like you."

"I'm not much for groups."

"You're a good soldier, Chains. I'd love to—"

"No." I put all my will into the word. "Thanks, Perfect, but I'd just drag you down."

Irritation flashes across Perfect's face, but his charming smile banishes the flutter in my stomach. "I disagree, but I respect your choice. Shoot me a private message if you get tired of the solo life."

"Thanks. I'll keep it in mind."

"Make sure you get off the street tonight. I'd hate to see someone with your talent die in his sleep." Perfect tips his top hat, saunters through the gate, and melts into the crowd.

His morbid parting words remind me I've got nowhere to sleep. As dusk falls over Geartown, I set off in search of shelter for the night.

———

31

CHAPTER 6

ROUGH NIGHT

The streets empty as the sky fades to bruised purple. Player groups shuffle into shabby wooden homes. Couples and solitary inmates converge on larger buildings whose signs depict ale tankards and beds. I pick one of the latter and push through the front doors.

The capacity crowd's droning banter rises to the high rafters. I shove my way through the booze-sodden common room. A pretty girl in a white apron stands smiling behind the wide oak bar.

"Hello there, traveler," she greets me. "What can I get you?"

Traveler. "Are you an NPC?"

She cocks her head. "I'm sorry, traveler, I didn't understand that."

"Right. Sorry." I feel awkward for having asked and even more awkward for having apologized to a computer program. "I'd like a room for the night."

"Standard rooms are five copper. Deluxe rooms cost two silver. The royal suite is one gold piece."

"What's the difference?"

"The deluxe room comes with more comfortable bedding and a complimentary meal. The royal suite includes these plus a heated bath."

"Just the standard, then." I hand her a coin and get a system message that I've lost one silver piece. "Got change?"

"Just a second." She closes her hand over the silver coin and hands back five coppers. I pick them up and crush them in my fist. Floating text tells me I've added five coppers to my inventory.

The barmaid passes me a fancy iron key. "You can access your room for twenty-four hours. Up those stairs to your left. You'll know it when you see it." She graces me with another bright smile. I crush the key into my inventory, turn on my heel, and head upstairs.

"Hey there." A brunette beauty in a tiny black dress blocks my path halfway up the steps. Her dark eyes smolder as she looked me up and down. "Need some company?"

"Nice dress you're almost wearing. No, thanks."

"A girl's gotta eat." She pouts. "Share the wealth. I'll make it worth your while."

"No." I shove past her and continue up the steps.

"Whatever, creep. Die in a fire."

The stairs lead to a rustic hallway with wooden doors on both sides marked **Locked**. I scan them until I find one labeled with my name in green text. The handle opens easily. I enter and swing the door shut. Despite the absence of a visible lock, the key gave me automatic entry, so hopefully it denies unwanted visitors.

Now entering player-owned safe zone flashes across my vision. **No hostile actions may be performed against the owner.**

That answers that.

My safe zone amounts to four walls and a shoddy bed with a patterned quilt. Night bird cries filter through the tiny window. Exhaustion washes over me. I stumble toward the bed but stop when I remember I'm still wearing my adventuring gear.

I pop my menu and contemplate unequipping everything until I spot a button marked **Sleep mode**. I press it and get another message: **This mode will remove all current gear and equip designated sleep gear. You may be vulnerable without your current gear. Continue?**

I scan my armor stats and attack values in the sidebar. Everything is based on my gear, so sleep mode takes me down to zero. Fatigue drives

CHAPTER 6 - ROUGH NIGHT

me to trust the safe zone message. I press **Continue**. My clothes and weapons dissolve into white light, leaving me butt naked.

"Hey, what kind of pervs designed this game?" I reequip my **Rough Pants**. At least I won't be swinging free in an unfamiliar land.

I climb into the coarse sheets. The simple quilt has a comforting heaviness that helps me drift off.

Thoughts of my mom and sister swirl through my mind before darkness takes me.

• • • •

The Second American Civil War drags on. Having lowered the age of consent to fourteen, the People's Republic of California extends the draft to females. Recruitment drives call on teen girls to strike a blow for equality. Those who come home get just enough disability to make them wards of the state.

Your new limbs are almost as good as your old ones, soldier. Make sure to thank the Party in your suicide note.

Enemy forces carpet-bomb a PRC charge. Plasma thunders from both sides, superheating the air into a lung-searing miasma. Teenage girls and boys lie bleeding from ragged stumps as the survivors fall back to trenches domed with crackling energy fields. Nobody wants to brave the cratered no-man's land.

Into this nightmare step the Reclaimers. Bearing winged, snake-entwined staffs on their gray fatigues, they wade unarmed through muck that reeks of burned pork.

In the middle of the battlefield, Sergeant Riley wipes black, filth-smeared hair from his dark eyes. He crawls hand over hand toward a dark-skinned girl lying in a pool of red mud. Only charred stubble remains of the raven curls that were her pride. Her uniform hangs on her elfin frame like a scarecrow's tatters.

The sergeant pulls himself past a mound of steaming meat to reach the girl. With practiced movements, he yanks a flesh patch from his chest pocket, strips the membrane, and slaps it on the bleeding stump of her right arm. It seals the wound and pumps morphine through the girl's system. Her sobs turn from agonized to terrified, and the Reclaimer cradles her bristly head against his shoulder.

"It's OK. You're not alone."

The girl clutches at him with her remaining arm. "Please don't leave me. Please don't leave me!"

"I won't. I'm gonna get you home. What's your name?"

"S- Sara."

"OK, Sara. I need you to help me. Can you do what I say?"

"I . . . think so." Her teeth chatter so hard, Riley fears they'll crack.

"We're gonna crawl back to our line," he says.

"I can't crawl. My arm . . ."

"I know. So here's what we'll do. You lay down next to me and wrap your other arm around mine. I'll drag us both home. Can you do that? Just hold on to me?"

"Y- yes. Please don't leave me."

"I won't. Just wiggle around till you're on your belly facing our line. Come on, I'll help you."

A bomb erupts nearby, and Sara flinches like a startled rabbit. She tries to sit up, but Riley yanks her back to the mud an instant before a plasma beam scours the air above their heads.

"Stay down!"

"I'm sorry," she wails. "I'm gonna die!"

Riley rolls Sara onto her belly, seizes her good shoulder, and maneuvers them both to face the PRC bunkers.

"Hold on," he grunts.

"Please don't leave me!" She clings to him like a baby, just like his little son does before Riley heads out on every tour.

Riley drags little Sara through the gore and mud inch by inch. She buries her face against his muscular arm as they pass heaps of flesh that were her friends. The Reclaimer keeps his eyes peeled for mines and sharp debris that might injure his charge.

The passage through hell seems to stretch on forever. Another bombing run misses them by sheer luck. Sara screams as scorching earth rains down, but Riley keeps moving.

At last, the Reclaimer's hand sparks against the shimmering dome over the PRC trench. The chips in their necks let him and Sara through without frying them. A medical squad carries her off, and Riley slides down the earthen wall into the pit.

"Rest easy, Sergeant," a medic says. "You're back with friends."

Riley takes the canteen the young man hands him, gulps down warm coppery water, and gasps.

"You're a hell of a man, Sergeant."

"Just another day on the job." Riley looks past the soldiers to pierce me with his dark gaze.

"If only my son were a tenth of the man I needed him to be."

My groceries lie spilled in the shag carpeted hallway. I'm running for the white bedroom door at the end, but the air turns thick as mud. Light seeps from the narrow crack, along with the rhythmic smacking of meat.

"No," my sister screams. "Please stop! No!"

Finally I reach the door and bust it open to see—

• • • •

I pitch out of bed with a ragged scream. My head bounces off the bare floor two feet below with a loud crack, and I lie there tangled in my itchy quilt. I choke on rapid breaths as the dream spins through my aching head.

"Dammit! Dammit! Dammit!" I pound the floor and get an **Indestructible Object** message each time my fist hits the hardwood. My curses devolve into lung-emptying screams. I heave a deep breath into my burning chest and vent again.

Stamina increased.

My breathing goes back to normal like somebody flipped a switch. Everything is a game here, even my pain.

Especially my pain.

Shit.

I collapse onto my back and stare at the cracked ceiling. How many times have I had this same dream? Maybe every night since I was arrested.

It never gets any easier.

I haul myself off the floor, open my menu, and reequip all my gear. "I need to go kill something."

My inventory argues with my bloodlust. No potions. Shoddy starting equipment. Necessity wins. I'll get myself killed if I don't tend to the basics.

My stomach rumbles right on cue.

"Dammit."

CHAPTER 7

SHOP LIKE YOUR LIFE DEPENDS ON IT

It's disgustingly early when I shamble downstairs. Only the NPC girl behind the counter populates the common room. She waves at me like she's already had six cups of coffee shot into her veins.

"Cryoblend developers must be morning people, huh?"

She angles her head in adorable confusion. "I'm sorry, traveler, I didn't understand that."

"Never mind. Where can a guy get a bite to eat?"

"We offer breakfast for just two coppers, traveler. Would you like some?"

"Sure, hit me."

I belly up to the bar. She reaches under the counter and pulls out a steaming platter of eggs with sourdough toast. I fork over the coins as she drops a spoon on the varnished countertop beside the loaded plate.

The eggs are the perfect blend of fluffy and cheesy. Juice runs down my chin as I savor the first heaping bite. The toasted bread has a pleasantly sour, oven-fresh taste enhanced by the dollop of whipped butter on top. I shovel food into my mouth until my stomach threatens to burst.

"How can computer data taste so damn good?"

"I'm not sure what you mean, traveler, but I take it you enjoyed the meal."

"Man, I'm stuffed to the gills. I hope I can walk out of here." The good food is threatening to wash away my nightmare-induced funk. "How can I be full when I'm eating data?" My foul mood surges back. "How can I be dreaming when I'm already asleep?"

"I'm sorry, traveler, I didn't—"

"Don't worry about it. I need to head out, but my gear is trash. Where can I get some armor and potions?"

"Most traveler-run shops are closed this time of morning, but some local establishments near the front gate open early."

I take this to mean the NPCs are early risers. Leave it to a server full of social outcasts to sleep in and miss the first sale of the day.

"Thanks for the grub."

"Of course. Return any time, traveler." Her excessively cheerful smile actually brightens my spirits. *How many male inmates haven't had a woman smile at them like that in years? I've had my mom and sister, but—*

My brain slams that door before the black mood creeps back in.

"Dammit. I need to kill something."

I head to the city gate where Perfect and I grabbed our goblin quest. Shops stand against the mighty wall like suspects in a lineup. The players swarming the street hid them from me yesterday. Signs hang above the shop doors, each painted with a picture: a suit of armor, a potion bottle, a loot bag, crossed swords.

I try the loot bag shop first. It's musty and cramped with shelves packed full of weird trinkets. An elderly vendor mans the counter.

"Hey, old man, I need to trade in fifteen goblin teeth. You paying?"

"Of course, traveler. I'll take anything you pull off those wretched beasts."

A trade window pops up, along with my inventory. I drag and drop the fifteen goblin teeth to my trade slot, and he ponies up thirty silver coins.

"That as good as you can do, gramps?"

"Prices are set by the royal family, boy. Don't like it, complain to them. Other travelers may pay you more if you want to hunt down a buyer."

"I didn't know NPCs could sound snide."

"I'm sorry, traveler, I didn't—"

"It's a deal, gramps." I click **Accept** and get a chime and a message that I've received thirty silver coins. I decide to hold on to my extra shield and the iron gear for now.

Next stop is the armor shop across the narrow street. Three players in red armor and full-face helmets march out together. Their names read **TRexFromSpace**, **TacoKing**, and **Chainsawlogy**. That last one holds the door for me. I nod in thanks as I slip inside.

A scent of metal polish mixed with oiled leather hangs in the air. An armor hoard of every type and material gleams in the candlelight.

"Good morning, traveler." The busty redheaded proprietor greets me from behind a wide back counter. "Looking to fortify your defense?"

"Who makes all these?"

"My husband and his brothers. Our family's been making armor for ten generations."

Or a week, whichever came first.

"I don't know exactly what I'm looking for. I just know these starting rags aren't gonna cut it anymore."

"Understood, traveler. What's your fighting style?"

"I bash the hell out of people with my shield. When they fall down, I stab them in the guts."

Saying that in the real world would get me locked up in a mental hospital, but she doesn't even bat an eye.

"Shields typically pair well with heavier-class armors, unless you're looking to maintain your agility."

"I'm not hopping around, if that's what you're asking. Take the hit, give back twice as hard."

"In that case, I recommend this section over here." She taps the counter twice in quick succession and gestures to a chunk of the wall holding chainmail and iron bracers. A window opens with a selection of goods separated into tabs.

"These upgrades are insane. Just upgrading my chest piece takes my armor rating from eight to forty?"

She puffs out her ample chest with pride. "Our work is the very best. Put your life in our hands."

"I've got forty-nine silver and some change, but I'll need potions and a weapon, too." I'm level 6. The cheapest upgrades require level 5, and the next step up requires level 10, so it's a no-brainer.

Chain Mail Shirt acquired.
Chain Mail Pants acquired.
Iron Greaves acquired.
Iron Bracers acquired.
Sturdy Belt acquired.

"Got anything better than this Goblin Tooth Shield?"

"That's probably the best item for your current level, traveler."

I drag the five new items into my equipment slots and press **Equip**. My outfit shimmers and transforms me into an iron badass. The chain mail clinks softly as I twist around to admire myself. The best news is that my armor rating jumps to 179.

"Killer. Thanks, babe."

"Anytime, traveler. Don't get killed out there."

Next stop, potions. The apothecary shop smells like mint and garlic. I double-tap the white counter like the busty armor vendor did, and the menu opens. Not knowing exactly what I'll need, I grab five health potions and two antidotes.

"It's gonna be a pain rummaging through my inventory for these during battle," I mutter.

"Put them in your quick slots, traveler," the crusty old witch behind the counter cackles. She jabs a bent finger at my waist.

My new belt has a pouch up front, sort of like a medieval fanny pack. I drop two health potions in there.

Quick slot 1 filled.
Quick slot 2 filled.

Last stop is the weaponsmith. My cutlass kills goblins OK, but an upgrade would butcher them faster. The bushy-mustached man in the back just nods at me before going back to grinding a sword on a wheel. The whole place smells like an old lighter that won't strike.

I tap twice to open the weapon progression chart. My cutlass lies at the base of the saber tree. Only one upgrade fits my current level and funds.

Toothed Saber acquired.

I equip the new weapon and pull it from my belt. "This looks vicious. Do all these barbs deal extra damage?"

The mustachioed craftsman keeps his eyes on his work. "Shreds the flesh. Hard to keep fighting when you're torn to ribbons."

"That's a little horrifying. But thanks."

Upgrades done, I exit the shop. I've got two silver and three coppers left in my inventory. Enough to eat and sleep tonight if hunting goes south.

The dark mood haunting the back of my mind since my nightmare swirls through my brain. I picture my dad, dead all these years. What would he think of me now? I wonder what my mom's going through with her only son in prison. My paychecks kept food on the table. And my sister—

"I don't want to think about that!"

I seize my hair with both hands and yank hard. The pain forces the image of her blood-spattered bedroom into its dank little corner. I yank a few more times until the physical pain blots out my mental agony.

The moment the intrusive images let up, I charge out the front gate. The same gate guard is still on watch.

"Hey, guard. I need to kill goblins. You recruiting again?"

"Ah, traveler. If you need the coin, Her Majesty's army could use your assistance—"

"I'll do it." I punch **Accept** on the quest window.

"Good hunting, traveler."

I sprint down the dirt road. Even in the heavy chain mail, I feel like I could run for hours. The only indications I'm exerting myself are the slow depletion of my stamina bar, just under my health bar, and the occasional notification.

Athletics skill increased to 10.

I reach the forest in a few minutes and halt just outside to let my stamina recover.

That hallway.

The light, the sound.

My sister screaming.

I charge into the forest.

Is it good luck or bad luck that I run into a small goblin patrol right away? Just two of them. But yesterday, two goblins nearly killed me. The pair pull their machetes with clockwork hands and leap at me.

"Come at me, you bastards. I'm not the same weakling I was!"

I swat the first goblin from midair with my toothy shield. His health bar drains by 30 percent as he tumbles into the murky shadows under an oak tree.

The second goblin slashes at my stomach, but I jump back and kick him in the face with my new iron boots. His teeth shatter in a spray of red pixels, and his health drops by 20 percent.

Sunbeams slanting through the canopy glint from my toothed saber as I drive it into the goblin's scalp. The spines rip through him easier than my cutlass with a bigger spray of red pixels. His health collapses to 10 percent as he scrambles backward on his butt.

The first goblin slashes my ankles while I'm distracted. Hot pain lances through my legs, but my health bar only drops 10 percent.

I kick goblin one in the eye. He screams as his health drops to 50 percent.

I'm back in Sis's bedroom. My fist aches, and droplets of warm blood spatter my face as I punch again. I cut my knuckle on my victim's tooth, but I don't care. I just keep pounding away. The rhythmic smacking of meat reminds me of another recent sound, and my rage boils over. Someone grabs my arm but can't stop me; no one can stop me.

I'll never stop.

It will never be enough.

Two piles of red glass carpet a murky forest floor. I gulp down heaving breaths of damp air as I scoop up two small brown bags and crush them in my fist. Sword and shield at the ready, I press deeper into the dark wood.

The lone goblin on the path doesn't see me coming. I split his half-brass skull with my sword, bash him to the ground with my shield, and stab him in the spine. The three attacks reduce him to red glass that splashes my new boots.

Thud. Thud. Thud.

"Please, I didn't mean to hurt her!"

Thud. Thud.

"She wanted it!"

Thud.

Crack.

Splash.

An arrow sprouts from my throat. It doesn't impair my breathing, but my purple health bar dwindles. I choke the goblin archer in the bushes with my left hand as I repeatedly ram my serrated blade into his guts. He squeals and sprays red glass all over my face.

You reached Level 8!
Now able to equip gear requiring level 8 and below.
Health and Stamina increased.
Skill rank caps increased to 80.
One-handed Swords skill increased to 70.
Shields skill increased to 70.
Heavy Armor skill increased to 45.
Brawling skill increased to 70.
Athletics increased to 70.
Intimidate skill increased to 57.
Perception skill increased to 60.
1125 XP gained.

I yank the arrow from my throat, pull an antidote from my pouch, and chug it in one go. The vial shatters into white pixels as another goblin hobbles toward me on steam-piston feet.

"Come get some, bitch."
It's not enough. It will never be enough.
Red glass.
That terrible bedroom.
That meat sound.
Splash.

You reached Level 10!

"Donovan, help me! Make him stop!"
"Come out and dance, you green vermin! You scared of me?"

You reached Level 12!

"If only my son were a tenth of the man I needed him to be."
"Dammit!"

You reached Level 14!
Now able to equip gear requiring level 14 and below.
Health and Stamina increased.
Skill rank caps increased to 140.
One-handed Swords skill increased to 130.
Shields skill increased to 130.
Heavy Armor skill increased to 100.
Brawling skill increased to 130.
Athletics increased to 130.
Intimidate skill increased to 100.
Perception skill increased to 100.
6125 XP gained.

Stamina depleted. You will need to rest until the Stamina bar is full.

An awful weight grinds me to one knee in a field of red glass. Feels like I'm trying to breathe underwater while fire rages through my veins.
It's still not enough.
It will never be enough.

My stamina recharges to one-third. The blackness fogging my mind thins. My health bar's down to 5 percent.

With numb fingers, I fish a health potion from my pouch and gulp it down. The taste of sweet peaches shakes off the madness that gripped me all morning.

"I'm a mess." My feeble punch barely dents the soft earth. "How does Perfect think I can help anyone when I can't even help myself?"

My stamina bar slowly fills back to max. The weight lifts from my shoulders, only to crush my heart.

"I'm no good like this. Anyone I take up with is just gonna get hurt. It's better if I—"

A woman's piercing scream cuts through the forest. I reflexively jump to my feet but freeze before I take a step.

"Dad's right, Chains," I mumble. "You're no hero." I hang the shield on my back and slip the sword into my belt.

Another scream—this time a long, keening note that's abruptly choked off.

I'm a kid again, staring up at my dad in his gray Reclaimer uniform.

"Daddy, why do you have to go?"

His smile holds no judgment. *"People need help, Donovan. I have to help them."*

"Why?"

"Because it's the right thing to do."

"I screwed up, Dad. I know I can never make you proud. Not after . . ." I grit my teeth. "But I'll be damned if I make you any more ashamed of me."

I dash through the dark forest to find the screamer.

CHAPTER 8

AN OFFER ACCEPTED

Black trees flash past as I sprint through the forest. Shouts, jeers, and metal ringing on metal grow louder. My palm throbs as I clutch my saber's hilt in a death grip.

I burst into a clearing overrun with Copper Hoods. Twelve of the cowled thugs circle four women standing amid a pile of green glass.

AznMischief, a petite dagger wielder in snug black leather, fights back to back with tall, curvy **MechaKarma**. Rippling muscles strain Karma's greasy coveralls as she swings a rusty pipe wrench. Three Hoods probe the mismatched duo's defenses with long, tapered blades.

Four more thugs rush in, separating a raven-haired warrior, **EnchantedBlizzard**, from her party. A knife to the chest leaves her with a sliver of health.

"Enchanted!" **HeartAtHome**'s auburn hair and green dress fan out as she twirls to slash the Hood that stabbed her friend. Her rapier drops his health to 30 percent. He retreats with a curse, but two more thugs push her to within ten feet of me. Her half-empty health bar hangs before my face.

I charge Heart's opponents, slashing and stabbing. Both Hoods run screeching like goblins. Heart aims a rapier thrust at me, but I raise my open left palm and point behind her with my saber. "No!"

Heart glances over her shoulder as a Copper Hood spears EnchantedBlizzard through the back. The barbed point erupts between her breasts in a spray of red pixels.

Enchanted drops her sword and fumbles at the spike jutting from her sternum. Her nineteen-year-old body disintegrates into tinkling green glass.

HeartAtHome screams.

I meet the murderer's leering eye through the glittering cloud and bare my teeth. "ChocolateReaper, you bastard."

"You seem upset." Reaper flicks his ponytail over his shoulder and hands the spear to a toady on his right. "Was she a friend of yours?"

I draw my shield and whack it with my blade. "I'm gonna stomp your back-stabbing ass into paste."

Reaper raises his hood and draws a pair of gear-studded maces. "Come get some, BrokenChains."

I stalk toward Reaper. Two thugs leap at me from his flanks. I've got my hands full just blocking their flashing blades, never mind counterattacking.

More Hoods join in, circling me like jackals. A few of their strikes slip through and take me down to 70 percent health.

Through it all, ChocolateReaper's roaring laughter assaults my ears.

HeartAtHome presses against my back. Her quivering is noticeable despite our combined layers of armor.

"What are you doing?" I shout.

She stabs at an encroaching Hood. "They murdered my friends!"

"I know." I barely parry a sword thrust aimed at my face. "That's why I bought you time to run."

"We ain't running, stud." AznMischief somersaults between two startled thugs to land on Heart's right with daggers ready. "Not till we teach these scumbags some manners."

"Save the lessons for later," I yell. "We need to clear a way out of here."

"Okaaaay!" Two thuds send a pair of Hoods hurtling from my left. I duck under them as MechaKarma comes bouncing toward our group. The circling jackals scatter before her swinging wrench.

"Follow me." I hunker behind my shield and run at the Copper Hood in front of me. His blade glances off my shield, and the spikes crunch into him. His health plummets to 20 percent as he goes flying.

ChocolateReaper steps aside to let the body sail past.

With the way open, I seize Heart's upper arm and throw her forward. "Run! Don't look back!"

Heart's long legs pump beneath her lacy battle skirt as she leads her party into the dark forest. She and Mischief run like deer, while Karma keeps up with long strides. I lag behind to play thug speedbump. If that's all I'm good for, so be it.

Reaper points a geared mace at me. "Kill him." A feral grin splits his cowled face. "And the women."

The Hoods form a wedge and close in. I slash the first punk who gets too close across his eyes. He shrieks and falls back as **Blinded** appears above his head. I think it's a temporary status effect, but I wish I could make it permanent.

I rush after Heart, Mischief, and Karma. The Copper Hoods surge after us. Their howls and jeers fill the forest.

The fastest runners catch up and plunge their longswords into my back. My health drops 10 percent, and I slash at them over my shoulder. My wild swings force them back and earn me some breathing room.

That room shrinks fast. The Hoods chew me down to 50 percent health, then 40. My stamina bar drops even faster. When the last 20 percent runs out, I'll be doubled over gasping for breath as the Copper Hoods surround me.

Why am I risking my life to save prisoners?

"People need help, Donovan," Dad whispers from the depths of my memory. *"It's the right thing to do."*

A rock outcropping rears up from the trees ahead. I steel myself to make a final stand. At least that will give Heart and the others time to escape.

"Sorry, Dad. This is how it ends. I never made it up to you."

I clamber up the thirty-foot rock. Twelve adventurers in shining armor gape at me from the other side. PerfectBlade sits in their midst, his long coat pooled on the ground. His open-mouthed stare pivots from me to Heart and her party, who skid to a halt on his left.

"Perfect," I gasp. "Copper Hoods. Coming to kill us!"

Perfect leaps to his feet and yanks his dual sabers from his belt. "Knights of the Golden Dawn, form a line!"

The gleaming Knights close ranks. A dark-skinned man in mismatched armor steps up beside Perfect, nocks a black arrow in a recurve bow, and takes aim.

I dive off the rock just before the Copper Hoods crest it. Heart, Mischief, and Karma join the Knights' line as I hit the grass and roll toward them.

ChocolateReaper stands atop the rock, surveying Perfect's crew.

I lurch to my feet and stand with the Knights. My voice shatters the fragile silence. "Sixteen to twelve, asshole!"

Reaper's mouth curls in a sneer beneath his hood. His companions form a blade-barbed semicircle around him.

"You seem upset, Reaper," I taunt him. "Come get some."

Reaper smacks his palm with one clockwork mace. "I'll come for you, Chains. Don't doubt it."

Perfect's mismatched archer fires a shot into the grass at Reaper's feet. The arrow explodes in a cloud of stinging shrapnel, and the Hoods dance like the ground's electrified.

"Scurry back to your hole." Perfect's sharp voice slashes through the Hoods' shouts.

Reaper gives me a parting glower before he and his men withdraw behind the hill.

Perfect sheathes his blades. The Knights return to their makeshift camp, spread blankets on the grass, and lay out various food items.

"Ooh, they're having a picnic." Karma's dark curls bob as she skips into camp, pulling a grumbling Mischief after her.

I avoid the crowd. So does Heart. Red rims underline her eyes, and she still holds her rapier poised. I sheathe my saber and ease toward her with my hands raised. "Mind if we talk?"

Her nostrils flare, but at length she nods. "Thank you for saving me."

"Sorry about your friends. Were you close?"

Her shoulders slump, and she finally sheathes her blade. "I met Enchanted Blizzard and BeautyInTheEye three days ago. Enchanted taught me the rules of this game and how to survive. She was a hardcore gamer before . . ." She sweeps her arms around.

"Before she got thrown in this digital prison," I finish for her.

"She deserved a better end." A sob breaks through her hard façade. "Enchanted and Beauty, both murdered in a video game. And for what?"

To entertain the people of California and pay their debt to society. "Why did those thugs go after you?"

"They wanted to press us into *service*. We refused. More forcefully than they expected."

"Kicking a mad dog won't stop it from mauling you. I get it."

Her shoulders tremble with the effort of holding back tears. When the shaking subsides, she lifts her glistening blue eyes. "We just wanted to find our way out of this death game. I was the weakest. Why did I survive?"

"Don't ask me, lady. I've got no plan and no hope. Talk to the hero."

Perfect strolls up to us. "I prefer to think of myself as a concerned citizen. What happened?"

"The Copper Hoods ambushed Heart and her party. Bastards had already killed one." My gaze drops to the ground. "I couldn't save the other girl."

"The Copper Hoods would feed on each other if they ran out of victims. All the dregs unfit for decent guilds fall into that crab bucket." Perfect bows to Heart from the waist, the very image of a gentleman. "My condolences on your loss. At least you have other companions."

Heart wipes her eyes. "I'd never met Karma and Mischief before those Hoods tried to press-gang us today."

Perfect's courtly tone darkens. "You humiliated the Hoods. They'll be out for revenge. You'd be safest grouping with us."

I sigh. "Like I told you before, I don't play well with others."

"This is life and death now, Chains. You walk away from us; they'll hunt you."

"Yeah, but—"

"Please, Chains." Tears trickle down Heart's face. I remember Mom and Sis crying in the courthouse. They're probably crying at home right now, if they haven't been thrown into the street.

"You're killing me." I rub my tangled hair. "I'm no good in groups. You guys can't rely on me."

"Why did you save me?"

Heart's question jabs me in the gut. Because I dishonored my father and crave to make amends, even though it's impossible.

Heart casts a nervous frown at my tensing jaw. "Why did you save me?" she asks again.

Dad's words tumble from my mouth. "It was the right thing to do."

Heart gives me a sad smile. "So you're just a hero, huh?"

"No." My voice cracks like a whip. Heart's eyes widen as she takes a step back.

"Don't get the wrong idea," I warn her. "Even an asshole can do the right thing now and again."

"You got that right, stud." Mischief saunters toward us from camp, munching on a sandwich.

Perfect motions from the waifish woman to the Knights dining behind her. "Since you've partaken of our board, I take it you're joining our ranks?"

Mischief scarfs down the last of her sandwich. "No chance, Honest Abe. We work alone."

Karma approaches to loom over Mischief and giggles. "No, we don't, silly. You and me are a team."

"I'm the brains, you're the stomach," Mischief grumbles. "Together we're one flawed mess. Come on, we're out of here."

"What will you do when the Copper Hoods hunt you down?" asks Perfect.

Mischief pauses three strides into her exit. "I been thinking about that. The crafting options have some explodey equalizers. Gonna put my trust in what my own hands can make."

"Me, too," Karma says with a grin.

"Whatever." Mischief waves to Heart. "Good luck, girl." She smirks at me. "See ya, stud." Both women disappear into the forest gloom.

Perfect turns to Heart with his arms folded. "Surely you can see the advantage in banding together."

Heart nods. "I won't let myself be a victim again. Count me in."

Hoping to escape notice, I turn to go, but Perfect grabs my shoulder. "She'll be safer with us *and* with you. Stick around and keep her safe. What do you say?"

I grind my teeth. Dad raised me to protect those weaker than myself, especially women and children. Perfect has my number, and he knows it.

"Fine, I'll join your crew. Don't blame me when the wheels come off."

A big grin spreads across Perfect's face. "Wouldn't dream of it. Welcome, Chains and Heart, to the Knights of the Golden Dawn."

"Thank you," Heart says. "I guess we're all in this together now."

My stomach sinks to my boots. It's only a matter of time until someone gets hurt on my watch. Then everyone will know how useless I am.

"Donovan, help me! Make him stop!"

I dig my nails into my palms to stop the memories.

Perfect just smiles.

CHAPTER 9

CHARMING
TROGLODYTES

I navigate Geartown's narrow streets as a crisp dawn breeze ruffles my hair. A gaggle of women in leather armor over linen gowns huddle on the corner up ahead.

"Did you hear?" A leggy blonde leans in to gossip with her wide-eyed conspirators. "Two more names appeared on the Dead Wall."

"Who was it?"

"EnchantedBlizzard and BeautyInTheEye. Cause of death: ChocolateReaper."

"Those are his third and fourth kills. No one I know wants to do business with him."

"Damned Copper Hoods. I hate them so much."

"I heard a player armorsmith refused to service Reaper a few days ago. Reaper ran him through."

"What a monster."

I pass the gossip squad and continue down the deserted street. Perfect's Knights have assembled in the big square near the front gate. I trudge toward them.

"Good morning, Chains." Heart breaks from the group and makes a beeline for me. Dark circles surround her puffy eyes.

Can't blame her. I wrestled with my own nightmares last night. "Morning. Sleep all right? You did watch two friends die."

She blinks. "Not exactly subtle, are you?"

"I can be, but it chafes me something fierce. You OK?"

"I'm . . . getting there. I only knew Enchanted and Beauty for three days, but people bond fast here. I'd be dead without them." She looks me in the eye. "I'd be dead without you, too."

"Don't sweat it. I'd do the same for anyone."

"I believe that." Her husky voice gets under my skin in the right and wrong ways.

"Listen, Heart, I meant what I said yesterday. You don't want to involve yourself with me. Sooner or later I'll screw up, and someone will pay the price."

"Is that what put you in here?"

I wince. "Look, I'm not your hero, OK?"

"No hero is coming to save me. I need to get strong so I can go home to . . . my family."

I let her suspicious pause go. "Everybody needs a reason, right?"

She nods. "Right. Thanks again for saving me. I owe you one."

"Oh, for the love of . . . Is that what this is about? Some kinda life debt?"

She frowns. "My father taught me about honor, Chains. I repay what I owe."

"You don't owe me jack."

"That's not true, Chains. I'm not leaving until I pay you back."

"Pay me back by leaving me the hell alone!"

Her cheeks puff up in anger. "You don't have to be an asshole. I'm trying to show you some gratitude."

"No, you're trying to tie yourself to my hip. When you get yourself killed, whose fault is it gonna be? I don't need another failure on my tally sheet."

"You're being a real jerk."

"And you're a stubborn—"

"Hello." A cheerful new voice intrudes on our shouting match. Heart and I turn from glaring at each other to glare at Perfect's dark-skinned archer. His face remains placid under our double-team death gaze, probably because he's looking at the space to the left of my ear instead of my eyes.

The nameplate above his head reads **Pu$$y_$layah_666**.

Heart's face goes blank. "No."

"No?" Slayah cocks his head. "No what?"

"Just no. What kind of name is that?"

"I've been assured it is a cool name."

"Ugh." Heart walks away. "Talk to me when you're done, Chains."

"Why do female players always react that way?" Slayah keeps staring at my ear. I resist the urge to fiddle with it.

"Seriously, dude?"

"Just what I want to see." Looking gallant in his top hat and frock coat, Perfect walks up and drops a hand on both our shoulders. "My walking encyclopedia and my new best friend, together already."

I furrow my brow. "Your walking what?"

"Chains, Slayah here is a genius when it comes to rattling off monster stats and designing combat strategies."

Slayah shifts his blank expression from my ear to the cobblestones. "It is nothing more than basic physics and memorization. You compare the monster's stats against your own, then arrange variables to maximize your potential—"

Perfect laughs and makes a sharp chopping motion. "We get it, Slayah. Save it for the battlefield, all right?"

Slayah pauses. "You want me to stop talking about it?"

"That's right."

Slayah silently inspects the stones under our feet.

Perfect slides his arm around my shoulders and guides me away. "He's a weirdo, but he's got a computer for a brain. You've met my left hand. Let me introduce you to my right."

We approach four dudes in shiny, fur-trimmed armor. **SquirrelOf-Death** clutches an iron spear and weighs me with beady eyes in a wide face. **LaserToast** spits onto the stones from the side of his goateed mouth. **HappySteak** polishes the round head of a mace with his dirty shirt. **Rainpig**, the biggest and ugliest, snorts as if at some joke. He traces Perfect's arm draped over my shoulder with his mean little eyes before locking them on mine.

"This is Chains." Perfect sweeps his hand around the group. "Chains, this is my right hand, Rainpig, and his squad."

"Charmed, I'm sure." I consider offering my hand to Rainpig, but I get the feeling he'd bite it.

The brute grunts at me and rolls broad shoulders with axe handles sticking up behind them. "Shield boy, huh?"

I grunt back. "Two axes, huh?"

"Cuts meat real good."

"That's adorable." I turn to Perfect. "What's the plan?"

"Good question." He drops his arm and hops onto a nearby fountain's lip to stand above the crowd. "Listen up. Prisoners of this sick game are dying as we speak. The Knights of the Golden Dawn won't stand for it. Our target today is the first-floor dungeon. We'll map it out quick as we can, find the boss, and take him down."

Murmurs of agreement pass through the gathering.

Perfect draws one of his sabers and holds it high overhead to catch the sun. "We'll clear this floor and bring hope to the people. Let's show them this game can be won. For the Golden Dawn!"

"For the Golden Dawn!" The twelve Knights repeat the guild motto.

Heart sidles up to me. "Feels like I joined a cult."

"Gotta rile up the troops somehow," I say.

Perfect thrusts his gleaming saber toward the front gates like a dashing young captain ordering a charge. "Onward, Knights. To battle! To victory! To eternal glory!"

CHAPTER 10

INTO THE DUNGEON

"**C**hains," Heart asks, "have you ever seen doors this tall?"

We stand in front of two giant doors set into the white marble cliff a few miles from Geartown. My mother took me to a museum in an old mansion once. The outside doors were ten feet tall. These are easily three times taller. Monster faces drawn with silver inlays cover the black wood.

"No." I press my ear to one black door. "Not even a sound. Who knows what's waiting in there?"

"Ask the walking encyclopedia." Heart frowns at Slayah. The archer stands a few feet away in consultation with Perfect, Rainpig, SquirrelOfDeath, LaserToast, and HappySteak. The other seven Knights wait behind them on standby.

"Most of these are skulls with gears embedded in them. There's no magic here, so I doubt we'll be fighting the undead. Then again, this is a video game."

"Listen up." Perfect's voice cuts through the chatter. All fourteen of us lock eyes on our fearless leader. "Behind these doors lies the first dungeon. We don't know what we'll face inside, so we need to stay on our toes. Those with shields and shorter weapons, man the frontline.

Anyone with polearms, fall in after them. Slayah, you're our only archer, so you'll be with me in the second rank."

Slayah raises his hand like a kid in grade school. A couple of the guys snicker, but Perfect gestures for him to speak.

"Should we designate a rear guard in case of ambush?"

Perfect catches himself rolling his eyes and puts on a serious face. "The monsters we've seen follow prescribed territorial patterns. We should expect the monsters inside the dungeon to do the same. If they don't, we'll recalibrate."

The Knights of the Golden Dawn form up. I take the rightmost position in the front row. To my dismay, Heart steps into line at my left.

"My interface shows everyone's partied up and looped into the raid group to share experience," Perfect says from the second row.

My nervous gaze sweeps from Heart beside me to Slayah and Perfect behind us. Their solid-green health bars float in my vision. I'd rather not have partied with them—or anyone—but our fearless leader insisted.

"Open it," orders Perfect. Rainpig, who's standing front row center, seizes the big silver handles on the leftmost door and pulls. The mammoth portal swings open with a groan. A black hole gapes before us.

"Torches." At Perfect's command, a couple of frontline Knights manifest torches from their inventories and activate them. The flickering light spills into the dungeon and reveals concrete floors spiderwebbed with ancient cracks.

"Stay alert," Perfect calls as we march into the darkness at his signal.

"Ah, man." I pinch my nose shut. "What's that stench?"

Heart's nose wrinkles. She reminds me of a puppy that's caught wind of a skunk. "It seems to be coming from all around us."

"You can't tell me this stink doesn't bother you, Heart."

"When you've changed a thousand dirty diapers, nothing fazes you."

"Diapers, huh? You got kids?"

She averts her eyes. "Let's just clear the dungeon, OK?"

"OK," I assure her. "I wouldn't want whackbag killers knowing about my family, either."

The frontline fighters take up defensive stances. Heart sticks close to me with her rapier drawn while I brandish my toothy saber and spiked shield.

"I need to upgrade my gear soon," I mutter to myself. "I leveled up pretty hard yesterday and didn't have time to replace it all."

"Don't hold us back with your trash-tier equipment, Chains." Laughter softens Perfect's harsh words.

I grin at the challenge. "Don't worry about me, Perfect. Just try to keep up."

"Don't let me step on your heels." His amused tone shifts back into command mode. "Spearmen, form the second rank around Slayah and myself. Take the kills you know you can get, but don't skewer our allies. Remember, we all share experience no matter who gets the kill, and we'll divvy up the loot later. Glory hounds and troublemakers get cut from the team."

Murmurs of assent rise from the group.

"Knights of the Golden Dawn," Perfect cries, "forward!"

I advance with the first rank. The spiderwebbed concrete walls and floor stretch to the edge of the torchlight. Shadows hide the ceiling.

Clattering echoes down the hallway a moment before skeletons charge from the darkness ahead. Brass fittings hold their bleached bones together. Gears churn inside their hollow rib cages, and scorching red lights burn from their eye sockets.

Heart lets out a shriek.

A skeleton swings his club at my head. I block the blow on my shield and slash at him, but my saber skitters off his ribs and only depletes a sliver of his health bar.

The other frontliners' slashing weapons barely scratch the undead, while the skeletons' clubs deal substantial damage, even through our armor.

I catch a skeletal fist to the side of the head. The punch sends me reeling as my health plunges to 70 percent.

"Skeletons have resistance against blades," Slayah drones over the clang of battle. "Use bludgeoning weapons."

"Crush them," Perfect shouts. "Smash them to bits!"

I lower my saber and raise my shield higher. When the skeleton comes at me again, I block his club and put all my weight into a shield bash. The impact vibrates my arm, but my foe's health falls 30 percent.

"It's working!" I bash again. The skeleton's health drops to zero. He crumbles into a pile of dust and whirring gears that sputter and die. The whole mess explodes into red glass.

"My rapier's useless," Heart grumbles. "What am I supposed to do?" She huddles behind my shield when the next skeleton's glowing eyes settle on us.

One large femur lies amid the red glass. I nudge it with my foot, and a nameplate appears: **Bone Club [Expires upon leaving dungeon]**.

I let my shield's straps support its weight on my arm and kick the club into my hand. "Use this."

"Ugh. I hate spooky dead things." Despite her protests, Heart sheathes her rapier and takes the femur. "It's lighter than I expected. Still, eww."

The next skeleton charges in. I bash him with my shield, and he reels back. Heart slams the femur down on his bleached skull, and half his health bar drains away. Before I can shield bash the skeleton again, Heart hammers his ribs. The undead crumbles and explodes into red glass.

Heart scans the empty corridor with a satisfied smile. "That was the last one."

"Pretty vicious swing, killer," I tease. "You play softball or do collections for the cartels?"

"I'm determined to get home." She grimaces at the femur. "Enough to bludgeon anything in my way with part of a dead guy."

The cracked walls echo with shambling footsteps. Slayah cocks his head at the sound. "Incoming second wave. Twice as many."

"Grab your loot bags and press on." Perfect hasn't engaged yet. I can't blame him since his sabers are about as useless right now as Slayah's arrows.

Metal clangs, and battle cries fill the tunnel as blocky robots swarm from the darkness and engage our frontline. One clockwork humanoid sidesteps my pistoning shield. "These bastards look bulky, but they're fast!"

Heart hurls the femur aside and gracefully draws her blade. She ducks under a robot's punch and pierces the ticking construct's metal stomach. Oil gushes from the puncture.

The wounded machine raises both arms and brings its steel fists down on Heart's head. My shield intercepts the blow, and she rams her blade into its head. Gears grind inside the robot. It slumps to one side and explodes in a sparkling red fountain.

"Blades work just fine," Heart shouts.

"Then here I come." Perfect leaps over the frontline to land between me and four encroaching bots. He dances through their formation, dodging their rigid blows and channeling his motion into fresh attacks. No movement is wasted as he ruptures their stomachs and slashes their heads.

All four bots crumble. Perfect strikes a pose on their red fragments and gives me a cocky backward glance. "How's that?"

The peanut gallery behind me explodes with cheers.

"That was amazing, boss!"

"Did you see him kill that fourth one with a flick of his wrist?"

"Just like a superhero!"

Perfect beams.

Slayah shoots an arrow over Perfect's shoulder and takes out an oncoming bot. "Might I suggest we save the celebration for after combat?"

"Gotta inspire the troops."

"I see skeletons blended in with the robots this time," says Slayah.

"Good eyes. Frontline, prioritize the skeletons if you've got the gear. Anyone who can't hit the undead should nail the robots instead. HappySteak, spread your mace damage around."

"Got it, boss!" HappySteak bellows.

"SquirrelOfDeath, your spear is useless up front. Stay in the second row, and hand out potions."

"Understood. Sorry, Perfect."

"Don't be sorry. Change your behavior and get some results. Rain-pig and LaserToast, you're solid. Keep up the brutality."

The two brutes grin like used car salesmen. "Heh. If you insist, boss," says Toast.

"You sure we need these other guys, Perfect?" Rainpig waves a meaty paw between me and Heart. "They seem kinda weak."

Perfect fights a smile. "Give them time to learn, Rain." He points his blade at the advancing foe. "Frontline, march on!"

"I'll show that greasy pig who's weak." Heart breaks from the line and lops off a robot's head with a flourish. She crunches through its shattered remains to close with the next target.

I double-time it to her side. A skeleton's rib cage cracks under my shield slam. Another stout whack glasses it. "Easy with the prima donna stuff, Heart. We've got to work together."

Slayah raises his monotone over the din. "Correct. The members of a strike team fit together like gears in a machine. It doesn't operate when components are out of place, or when one runs too fast."

"Can we not talk about gears right now?" Heart punctures another robot's gut and dodges the resulting oil fountain.

Slayah fires an arrow from ten feet. Hit shot pulverizes a robot's glowing red eye and sends it crashing to the floor. "Very well. What would you like to talk about?"

"This is not the time for chatting," Heart says as she dances away from a skeleton's mace. "Just tell us what to do."

"In that case, you should duck."

"What—?"

"Down!" Slayah's command sends Heart diving to the floor. His glowing arrow streaks through the space her head just occupied, lances through the robot standing behind her, and tags a skeleton shambling behind the robot. The arrow enters the skeleton's eye socket and shatters its skull in an orange flash. Both enemies explode into red glass.

"Whoa, Slayah!" Heart gasps. "What did you do?"

Slayah nocks another arrow. "Flair. A special ability unlocked with diligent practice of a skill."

I batter another skeleton to the ground and slam my shield's rim into its rib cage. It dies, leaving the area around me empty. Only one robot and one skeleton remain standing thirty feet away. "What skill rank unlocks special abilities?"

"It varies based on the skill," Slayah says as he scores a bullseye on the robot. "Archery rank four hundred unlocks Penetrating Burst."

"Four hundred? Slayah, you're already level forty?"

"I was when I unlocked that skill."

"Do you do anything but grind levels?"

Slayah shoots the last skeleton down and cocks his head in thought. "I also sleep and eat."

My stomach rumbles. "I could stand to refill my tank. And my health."

SquirrelOfDeath passes me a red vial. "You earned your keep, noob."

"Thanks." I bolt down some peach sweetness and toss the vial aside as my health bar refills to max.

"What level are you, Slayah?" asks Heart.

Perfect's casual tone takes a hard edge. "Slayah's the only Knight with a level higher than mine."

Slayah shrugs. "Consistent focus yields results."

"Put that focus to work." Perfect waves us down the glass-strewn tunnel. "Let's clear this dungeon."

"Our odds of locating and defeating this dungeon's boss today are statistically nil," says Slayah. "Based on resources expended and damage taken in this battle, our current survivability window is eighty minutes. I strongly suggest we tactically redeploy to rest and resupply."

Perfect frowns. "And waste our momentum? Weren't you just preaching diligence and focus?"

"I actually agree with him." Heart sheathes her rapier and collects a bag with her name on it. "All of us are hurt, and our potions won't last long at this rate. Heading back to town is the smart play."

Rainpig snorts. "If you can't take the heat, get back in the kitchen."

Heart advances on the brute, but I hold her arm. "Get your brain outta your stomach, Pigman." I look to Perfect. "My vote goes to Slayah."

Perfect stands quiet in the torchlight, his mouth a compressed line. At length he shrugs. "A good leader picks a smart team and heeds their advice." He turns his winning smile on the others. "Strong work today, Knights. We'll give the boss a one-night reprieve and reconvene here at five a.m. sharp."

CHAPTER 11

PREDATORS IN THE DARK

I bury my saber in a robot's copper guts. The finisher frags him, and red glass patters into the filth around my boots.

"Three days," Heart huffs. She blows a stray auburn lock off her forehead. "Three days of fighting in this stench."

"You said smells don't bother you."

"I didn't know we'd be crawling through a sewer! This is disgusting. Who puts a sewer in a video game?"

"Sewers are standard entry dungeons for new players." Slayah hunkers down nearby with his parchment, peering into the darkness.

"Perfect wants you mapping, not painting landscapes," I tease Slayah. "Whatcha looking for?"

"Rats," Slayah says flatly.

"Rats?" Heart glares around the flooded tunnel. "Are you sure?"

"Current game design doctrine dictates adding giant rats."

"Don't freak out, Heart." I grind the red glass underfoot into slush. "They're just digital."

"I don't care." Heart crosses her arms under her breasts. "I won't fight any slimy rats, digital or otherwise."

"I thought you were determined to get home."

Her eyes widen like I just slapped her. Then they harden to flint. "I will. I'll kill anything in the way of getting home."

"Even rats?" I grin.

Heart's cold eyes rake my face. "Anything. Rats, skeletons, or people. I'm getting home."

Perfect steps past us and surveys the empty battlefield. "Looks like we got them all. Hear any more coming, Slayah?"

"Not at this time."

The tunnel splits in three at the limit of my vision. "A crossroads."

Heart holds her nose. "And every path stinks."

"Three roads . . ." Perfect narrows his eyes at the left tunnel as if he can pierce the shadows. "Let's take a breather. Rainpig, LaserToast, pick a side of the camp and stand guard. The rest of you eat up, get your energy back." He stows his blades in his belt and manifests a sandwich from his inventory.

Heart's fair complexion turns green. "How can you eat in here?"

"Victory is the best seasoning. Have a snack because we're back on the clock in ten." Perfect strides down the left tunnel. "I'm gonna scout ahead."

I move to join him. "I'll come with you."

He waves me off. "I'm one of the highest-level players in the party. Let me handle the scouting while you rest up."

I shrug. "You're the boss."

Perfect shoots me a thumbs-up, takes a bite of his lunch, and strides into the yawning darkness.

Slayah tosses his lit torch on a patch of dry ground nearest the left tunnel and squats next to it. A few swipes of his fingers conjure a large burrito in his hand. Steam rises from the warm flour tortilla as he peels back the aluminum wrap.

My mouth waters. "Slayah, bro, that looks too good for this world. Where'd you get it?"

"A player-run restaurant on Greaser Avenue. Ugly Johnny's."

"Crap." I smack my grungy head. "Perfect told me about that place, but I forgot to try it. They any good?"

A joyful expression overtakes Slayah's neutral features. "They are *killer*."

"Urgh." I manifest my own lunch: a loaf of plain bread and some dried meat. "I've been grabbing lunch from the innkeeper. All she offers for long-term storage is travel food like this. How do they keep the burrito from timing out and getting the Rotten status?"

Slayah's got half the burrito crammed in his cheeks like a chipmunk, so he just points at the aluminum foil.

"Special wrap item? Dang, I should have thought of that. I bet Ugly Johnny makes a fortune feeding dungeon crawlers." I glance at my stale lunch again. "I'm heading there tomorrow. This crap just doesn't cut it."

"Um." Heart's tentative voice makes me turn around. "I brought extra today. Do you want to share?"

Her face coloration has swung back from sickly to slightly reddened.

Perception skill increased to 110.

"Sure," I say. "Anything's better than choking down this shoe leather. Whatcha got?"

"Grilled portobello Philly sandwich." Heart manifests an eighteen-inch tube of aluminum foil. The grilled onion and pepper aroma drives out the ambient stench. She rips the whole thing in half without unwrapping it and hands over my portion. "I hope you like it."

The aluminum burns my fingertips as I peel it back. Even before I get the sandwich in my mouth, the steam fills my nostrils with a tantalizing grilled-mushroom fragrance. I sink my teeth in and let the salty moisture burst on my tongue.

Heart's staring at me nervously. I shove another huge bite in my mouth and give her a thumbs-up. "Oh manf, thif if *goof*."

Her beaming smile lights up the tunnel. "I'm glad you think it's good. Cooking for one felt weird after years of serving a big group."

I swallow with a mighty gulp. "This is the best Philly sandwich I've ever had. You used mushrooms instead of meat?"

"They're cheaper." She shrugs. "We don't make enough for the premium ingredients yet. I can put chicken or something in it tomorrow."

"That smells good." Slayah glances between his burrito and my sandwich. "Chains, I propose a trade."

"Hmm." I bite another chunk of the sandwich and hand it over. "Deal. Just so you can savor the experience that is Heart's cooking. I doubt she'll cook for you, after all."

Heart brushes my comment off. "I don't mind. It's not like I hate him."

"Could have fooled me," I say.

"No. It's just . . ." Her face flushes from pink to beet red. "That *name*."

Slayah tears into the sandwich like a starving beast. "Oh manf, thif if *goof*."

"Right? I'm telling you, Heart, you should open a vendor's cart at the city gates. You'd make a killing." I sink my teeth into the burrito. Fluffy warm rice and soft beans caress my tongue as juicy carne asada overwhelms my taste buds. "Two miracles in one day. I could get used to this."

Heart laughs. "I don't mind cooking for both of you. Just pitch in for some ingredients, and I'll pack a lunch basket every day. But no cart. I can't afford any distractions from getting home."

"Believe me," I tell her, "I share the sentiment. Now that we've established I'm no scumbag, mind telling me what's waiting for you back in meatspace?"

"Be silent." Slayah hisses. He's laser focused on the right tunnel. He quenches the torch in the grimy water. The light of the other groups' torches doesn't reach us. Footsteps slosh down the side passage.

Too early to be Perfect and coming from the wrong direction.

Seconds tick by as the footsteps grow louder. The sudden flare of a torch reveals six figures. Each wears a copper hood.

I grip my saber so hard my palm aches, but the Hoods continue across the tunnel and into the left passage.

"Perfect went that way." Slayah's tense voice scrapes my nerves. He reactivates his torch to reveal his lips pursed in thought.

"Should we follow him?" I ask.

Slayah's eyes dart around as he calculates. He shakes his head. "We can track his health bar. If they attack him, we will know. Going now risks alerting them to our presence."

"Makes sense," I say. "But if he gets so much as a status effect, I'm heading in."

Slayah nods. "Agreed."

We wait in tense silence. Minutes later, Perfect comes swaggering out of the darkness.

"Dead end that way. I . . ." He stares at us in confusion. "What's wrong with you?"

I stand up and brush off my slime-stained pants. "Copper Hoods. Six of them followed you. Did you see them?"

His expression shifts so fast, I almost miss the fear that comes before his bravado. Knowing a squad of killers was hot on my heels would've shaken my cool, too.

"Copper Hoods? So that's who I heard splashing after me. I ducked down a side tunnel until they passed."

"Good thing. You're a tough bastard, but five on one sounds like a waste of resources." I shoot Perfect a grin.

After a beat, he grins back. "Yeah. Gotta save our potions for the mapping. Slayah, how's the dungeon map coming?"

"We have the southern portion cleared so far. Every side passage is accounted for. We need to thoroughly check these three tunnels and see where they go."

"I'm not leading a tour of the sewers. We just need to find the boss room."

"But mapping every strategic resource could prove useful in the future."

Perfect sighs. "Just make it fast. We need to be the first guild to clear this boss and give the people hope. Second place doesn't cut it."

"Hey." I drop my hand on his shoulder. "As long as we get home, it's all the same. Right?"

"No, it's *not* all the same." He shrugs my hand off. "Do you want the Copper Hoods to take the glory? That's a recipe for despair."

"Perfect, easy." I hold up both hands. "Your voice carries in these tunnels, bro."

"I'm just saying, we need to get this dungeon cleared fast. Slayah can map every dead end later." He stomps toward the center tunnel ahead of us. "Everyone up. Break time's over."

Rainpig shoulder checks me and lumbers after our leader. "Looks like someone's not his favorite anymore," he laughs.

"Not trying to be anyone's favorite, meathead."

LaserToast sneers at me as he follows Pigman. "Go play with your bimbo and pet android." He spits in Heart and Slayah's direction.

My boiling blood drives me toe to toe with LaserToast. "You got a problem? Let's settle it."

Toast's bearded lips pull back in a snarl. "I'll make you scream like the day you landed."

"Boys," Perfect shouts, "keep your pants zipped. Rainpig, Laser-Toast, take the right flank. Chains, you and Heart take the left."

The goons meanmug me as we gravitate to opposite sides of the line.

"They're gonna be trouble," Heart whispers in my ear. "They'll stick you in the back the first chance they get."

"Let them try." My leather gloves creak as my hands bunch into fists. "Let them try."

CHAPTER 12

A CHANGE IN PLANS

"**S**ix days, Slayah," Perfect shouts over the clash of battle ringing off the grimy sewer walls. "We've been down here six days!"

"By my calculations, we have completed at least half the map—"

"Don't tell me about your damn map!" Perfect tries to snatch the parchment from Slayah's hands, but the archer darts away.

As our leader and his left-hand strategist bicker like idiots, the front-line battles a wave of foes. I absorb a vicious blow from a skeleton's club. The hit rattles my newly purchased steel kite shield but fails to penetrate. Another smash from my matching steel mace crumbles the undead into crimson shards.

"I look like a chromed-out weirdo in all this steel gear, but it makes me feel bulletproof."

Heart glasses a robot with her clockwork rapier upgrade and turns to give me a once-over. "You look like a knight in shining armor."

"Watch out, digital world, here comes Prince Charming to plunder your sewer! Your outfit looks good, too. We clear this map, and all the starlets'll be rocking armored ball gowns on the red carpet."

Heart blushes. A skeleton looms behind her. I shout a warning, and she spins to parry its spiked mace. The monster takes a rapier thrust to both its red eyes before it crumbles.

"No mercy for those in my way." Heart spits at its pixelated remains.

Have you noticed they're getting tougher and better equipped?" I ask.

"I would have, if the sewer water wasn't up to my calves now." She grimaces at the pool of cold water flowing down the main chamber's center aisle. "At least we can avoid the water in some of the side passages."

Perfect turns from his argument with Slayah. "This would be easier if the water flowed from one direction. We could just trace it to its source."

"That assumes the boss room will be at the head of the flow." Slayah stares at Perfect's chest, but I've known the archer long enough to see the gears turning in his head. "It is possible the developers planned such a simple flow for the first dungeon, but we have seen so many branching passages, I suspect the boss room lies in a totally different direction."

Perfect jabs a slender finger at the archer. "And I'm telling you, stop worrying about every little room and get us to the boss!"

I say, stepping between them, "Slayah's side trips have netted us a ton of free loot. That last chest alone purchased all my equipment upgrades."

Perfect grinds his teeth. "If I need your opinion, Chains, I'll ask for it."

Tension crackles between us. The urge to knock his pearly teeth down his throat creeps up from my animal brain. Instead, I force myself to shrug. "You want us to keep following the main water?"

He holds me in a glare a moment longer, turns away, and growls in frustration. "Yes, but the damn river branches so many times, it's impossible to identify the main source."

"Let's compromise," I offer. "Form two teams and have each cover a branch until one group hits a dead end, then reunite and follow the other path. Slayah and I can scout the side passages. Two men won't draw huge mobs, and Heart can hold our place on the frontline."

Slayah cocks his head. "This is tactically sound."

Perfect throws up his hands. "Fine. Whatever gets me to the boss room faster."

"I crafted something just for this eventuality." Slayah manifests a clockwork sphere and hands it to me. Its ticking pulses in my palm.

"A robot grapefruit?" I ask.

He pulls a matching sphere from his inventory and speaks into it. "A communication device." His voice echoes from my sphere.

"Cool, walkie-talkies."

"Use this to stay in contact with the main group. Try scouting down that side passage to our left, and let me know what you see."

"Sounds good," I agree. "But if I get overwhelmed and killed, I swear I'll haunt you and your burritos forever."

"A curious thought. Do deceased players leave digital ghosts?"

"I don't wanna think about it." I shake my head and step into the darkness. "Catch you later, buddy."

• • • •

"Ah, it's good to be back in the sunlight!" Heart stretches her arms over her head as we return to town from another incomplete dungeon crawl. The city scent of coal smoke, rotten fruit, and sweat smells heavenly after the sewer's reek.

I kick a stray rock across the cobblestone street. "We've spent six days mapping that filthy sewer. By the end of a shift, I've almost forgotten what it's like to see the sky."

"Digital sky," Slayah corrects me.

"Sure, but it feels good to be out of the mines, right?"

He shrugs. "I have spent so much time in VRMMO dungeon delvers or alone in my room, the dark is home to me. All this bright light is unnatural."

"I knew it," Heart laughs. "You're a vampire."

Slayah cocks his head. "Vampire is not a playable character race."

Heart sighs.

I clap him on the shoulder. "You're a lost cause, buddy. That's fine. We're all a little crazy."

Slayah looks into space. "At least we got fifteen side passages mapped today."

Heart frowns. "Perfect was pretty mad we didn't find the boss room."

"'Pretty mad?'" I laugh. "When the river ended in that waterfall with a blank wall behind it, I thought he was gonna have a stroke. I damn near laughed out loud when he broke his favorite sword against the wall like a maniac."

Heart raises an auburn eyebrow. "I thought you guys were friends."

"We are." I mull it over. "We were. I don't know. He's really on edge lately. I don't like how he lays into Slayah."

"Rainpig and LaserToast seem to have it in for him, too."

"Is that unusual?" asks Slayah.

I bring us to a halt. "Why would you ask that?"

"Most people treat me that way."

Heart frowns. "We don't."

"You took umbrage at my name."

"We got off on the wrong foot," Heart admits. "But you're not so bad now that I've gotten to know you."

"Are you saying we are friends?"

She thinks it over, then smiles. "Yeah, I guess we are."

"Great, we're all pals." I throw my arms around their shoulders. "What do you say we grab some dinner? My treat this time."

"Ooh," squeals Heart, "I'll take buttered lobster and sushi on a golden platter."

"Scale it back," I deadpan. "Maybe a graham cracker with some peanut butter."

"I shall accompany you," says Slayah. "Should we try the burritos?"

"You read my mind, bro. Let's do it."

We grab burritos from Ugly Johnny's, a cramped dive decorated with monster trophies, and plop down on a low wall ringing the square to eat.

I swallow a savory mouthful. "This burrito satisfies me in ways I didn't know were possible."

"I eat three per day." Slayah takes another wolfish bite.

"You boys eat like lions stripping a zebra carcass."

"How can you pick at it like that, Heart? Burritos like this are meant to be scarfed."

"Excuse me if I have manners." She laughs and hands over a couple of napkins.

I mop my face. "Thanks. I can tell you're a mom."

She goes still. I'm about to change the subject when she relaxes. "Yeah. I have a child."

I set down my food. "Is that who you're fighting to get back to?"

"That's right."

"Don't wanna talk about it?"

"We're in prison." She gestures around the steaming city. "I don't know who to trust."

"Fair point. I'm not eager to talk about my past, either."

"What is so difficult about it?" Slayah tosses his aluminum foil on the flagstones. Three seconds later, it bursts into purple glass and dissolves.

"It's personal." Heart stares at him. "Doesn't it weird you out to discuss your private life with strangers?"

Slayah shrugs. "I am not particular."

I finish my meal and toss the wrapper. "I'm wiped out. You guys stay at the same inn as me, right?"

"We do." Heart stands up and brushes off her green skirts, though they're free of crumbs. She carefully folds the foil around her remaining burrito half and sets it on the ground to dissolve. "Lead on."

We stride through the streets as the sun sinks over the horizon. Geartown churns with the final daytime frenzy before people head inside for their nightly debauchery.

We're one block from the inn when ten Copper Hoods slip from behind some vacant wagons. They surround us in a tight circle with their blades pointed at our necks. I'm so stuffed and sleepy, I don't have time to yank my shield off my back.

ChocolateReaper lopes forward, a toothy smile glinting under his hood. "We're taking the archer. Don't resist."

Heart and I glance at our friend. Slayah's espresso face hardens. "If I refuse, you will harm us?"

"We'll kill your friends, yeah."

"Very well, I accept."

"Slayah, don't do it!" Heart's voice is frantic. "He murdered my friends. He'll kill you, too!"

"There appears to be no choice." Slayah raises his empty hands. "Lead on."

Two Hoods grab Slayah's arms, clamp manacles on his wrists, and drag him away. Memories of my sentencing send a hot jolt up my spine. But with blades at my throat, all I can do is watch them drag my friend into the falling darkness.

"You come after us, we'll gut you like rats." The hulking Reaper backs away. His troops follow, leaving Heart and me alone in the street.

CHAPTER 13

FRENZY IN THE DARK

"What do we do, Chains?" Heart demands. "What the hell do we do?"

"Give me a second to think." The weak light drenching our empty street fades to bruised purple, and in the eerie silence, our panting breaths drive my fear toward panic.

"I already lost two friends to those thugs, Chains. I won't lose Slayah."

"Let's calm down. We can't do jack for Slayah with half a working brain between us." I gulp down a breath and let the air flow out my nostrils. A few deep breaths ease the pressure on my pounding heart.

Heart's chest swells and deflates. "OK, we're calmed down. Now what?"

"Now we look for clues. We need to figure out where they went and follow them."

"They headed toward that alley there, behind that sweets shop."

"Then we follow. Keep your blade ready, Heart."

"I always do."

We slip into the shadow-drenched alley.

I point to four lines of footprints in the mud. "We're in luck."

Heart squints. "How did you see that in the dark, Chains?"

"I've been building my Perception skill. And as a kid, my . . . I learned to track. Four different sets of prints here, see?"

"Just barely."

"The guy on the middle left isn't leaving clear impressions. More like drag marks. He's forcing them to pull him and leave more noticeable tracks. Let's see where they go."

"Lead on," says Heart. "This place is a maze, and I'm practically blind."

I guide Heart down the network of winding back roads until more tracks join the group. "All ten of them reunited right here. Slayah's tracks disappear."

"Did they kill him?" Heart's genuine concern stokes mine.

"No. These two original sets suddenly get deeper. That means they're carrying him."

"The Hoods might've caught on to him. We should hurry."

The grungy alley ends in a wide brick street.

"Chains, this street is clean. The footprints end here. What do we do?"

"Let's check the other alleys and see where the footprints . . . Hold on, what's that sound?"

Masculine whispers grow steadily louder as Heart and I rush to a wooden crate on the side of the street. There, sparkling in the streetlamps' guttering light, sits one of Slayah's clockwork orbs.

"Pick up your damn feet, idiots." The gruff voice sounds distant. "This ain't the night for a pleasure hike."

"Where are you taking me?" Slayah asks, much clearer and more businesslike.

"You've been mapping the dungeon for that pansy PerfectBlade, right? Tonight you're gonna help us find the boss room."

"And if I refuse?"

"We kill you."

"I suppose I had better help you map the final dungeon, then. Have you spent much time in the dungeon? I suspect we will have much work to do tonight in the dungeon."

"Shut your hole! Damn, you're annoying."

"Can I talk again when we get to the dungeon?"

I grin at Heart. "Gee, where do you think he's headed?"

"I appreciate his obvious hints. I just hope he doesn't get himself killed trying to guide us."

Heart and I bolt through the main gate, past the guards, and up the road toward the far white cliffs. The communicator transmits the giant doors creaking open and slamming shut. Precious minutes pass before the silver-scrawled black slabs come into sight. We ease the doors open and slip inside the dark sewer like ninja mice.

"I've got my sword and shield to carry," I whisper. "Can you handle the torch?"

"Even better." She slides open her menu and manifests a nightlight in her palm.

"Is that a bunny? With a sword?"

"Damn straight. Isn't Fluffles adorable?"

"Fluffles?" Whatever his name, he gives just enough light to see by. "Let's just go."

"We are turning left?" Slayah's voice squawks from the speaker. "We went straight all this time, but now, after thirteen side passages, we are turning left? Why left?"

For once, Reaper drowns him out. "*Shut your damn hole!*"

I nod at Heart. "Let's book it. Straight down the main passage."

We run. Our footsteps echo in the empty sewer tunnel. Piles of red glass twinkle in the wobbling light of Fluffles, the bunny warrior.

"Just follow the trail of carnage, Heart."

"Never thought I'd be so happy to see monster remains."

"They're clearing the way, which means they're moving slower than us. OK, here's the thirteenth left."

Our boots grind through red glass as we turn.

"This is where your current mapping ends?" Slayah's voice holds a hint of surprise. "I also have not explored beyond this exact point."

"Stop yapping and start mapping."

"Understood. So, to recap our bearings, we took a left at the thirteenth left turn, a right at the second turn, and went straight for two intersections before turning right again."

"Don't tell me where we been; tell me where we're going!" The sound of steel hissing from a sheath silences Slayah's voice.

I fly down the dark tunnels, splashing through pools of fetid water. Heart matches my pace.

"Damn Hoods," Heart curses. "I should be soaking in a hot bath right now."

"I'm just glad these assholes avoided the flooded passageways."

Slayah's voice comes through again. "I see, so this tunnel leads to another dead end."

"Stop finding us dead ends, moron. Where's the boss room?"

"Failing to document the dead ends means our escape may prove perilous. If we panic and run, how will we recall the way to safety?"

"If we're in that much danger, I'll throw you to the monsters to buy time." A hard slap wrenches a cry from Slayah.

I grind my teeth. "Time's running out."

"Slow, slow," Heart pants. Her stamina bar is almost empty. I slow to a brisk walk beside her.

"Slayah lost twenty percent of his health, Heart."

"We can't help him if we're exhausted."

"I hate that you're right."

"The two of us can't beat ten of them, anyway. We need a plan."

"OK, let me think." The sparkling red glass leads left around another corner. Male voices echo down the tunnel, and Slayah's monotone answers. The distance muffles their words.

Whirs and clanks from the opposite way draw my attention to a cluster of bulky robots. We're outside their territory, so they just mill about in sparky agitation.

"Hey, Heart, I've got a really dumb idea."

"Great, I'm all ears."

"We both gather a couple groups of monsters. Don't attack them; just get their attention to draw minimum aggression. We kite them into the next tunnel and rush past the Copper Hoods."

"Kite them?"

"Lead them on. If we get lucky, some thug attacks a monster and draws instant aggro from the whole group."

"And we slip away with Slayah?"

"Bingo."

She bites her lip. "We're deep in uncharted territory, Chains. There's only one potion between us, so we'll have to be insanely careful about our health."

"If we pull this off, the monsters and the Hoods will be too busy fighting each other to chase us."

She fidgets. "Is this the only way?"

"Do you trust me?"

"Mostly."

"Heart, I've stuck my neck out for you since we met. You're why I joined Perfect's guild."

She scowls. "Don't pin your buyer's remorse on me."

"That's just it. I should regret joining, but I don't. Perfect was right; nobody gets out of here alone. So find someone to trust, or roll over and die."

Heart's graceful shoulders slump. "What do I need to do?"

"You take that robot cluster on the right. I'll go find some skeletons. That should get us about fifteen enemies."

Her furrowed brow smooths. "OK, Chains. I trust you." She steals into the dark tunnel, taking our only light source.

I delve deeper into the tunnel in search of skeletons. A chorus of clacking leads me to a band of undead. Fleshless mandibles snap shut as eight sets of red eyes fasten on me. Grabbing aggro usually feels like an electric jolt, but in the pitch-black nighttime tunnels, it's like a bolt of lightning running up my spine.

"I've got them!" Heart yowls from behind me. I spring into motion after her as my skeleton pursuers clatter over the spiderwebbed concrete.

"This was a really dumb idea, Chains," Heart pants as I pull alongside her.

"I told you it was."

Fluffles casts wavering shadows all over the tunnel as Heart and I lead fifteen surging monsters down the sewer toward the Copper Hoods. All ten of them mill around a side tunnel in a loose group. The thugs' voices rise in alarm at our approach.

———

We rush past the first Copper Hood before he can react. In a moment, we're deep inside the enemy formation. ChocolateReaper stands against the right wall like a massive shadow. He draws his maces and lurches toward us.

A single Hood has Slayah at knifepoint. The guard's narrowed eyes bulge as he stares past me to the onrushing monsters.

I yank my archer friend out of his captor's grasp and pull Slayah along. The Hood shouts as his blade scrapes on bone. The jolt running up my back vanishes when all eight skeletons focus on their new target and his allies.

I have just enough time to flash ChocolateReaper a middle finger before the three of us burst out the back of his formation. He glowers at me and barks frantic orders at his crew.

"Ah, excellent," Slayah murmurs as we charge into the darkness. "I had hoped my clues would prove sufficient to discern my location."

The sounds of battle fall away behind us.

I release Slayah's arm as I run. "No new monsters so far. That's good news."

"Indeed. Though I suspect it is only a matter of time."

"What are we gonna do, Chains?" Heart huffs. "If we stop to fight, they'll catch us."

"Or follow the red glass," Slayah adds.

"We'll need to kill as fast as we can, then move. Glass a few on side passages to create false trails."

"Understood."

"Let's do it!"

Fluffles's wavering light spills across four bulky robots tromping around the middle of our narrow tunnel. I break left while Slayah and Heart go right and charge past the monsters. Their blocky heads swivel to follow us as we bolt past. A shock runs down my spine.

I point left at five robots lurking in a narrow opening ahead. "Turn left up there. We'll kite them a ways before we kill them, so the glass isn't at the tunnel mouth."

I bash one of the robots with my steel mace for 20 percent of its health as we run by. Slayah and Heart take potshots of their own. Slayah scores a critical hit and almost drops his enemy in one shot.

"Too close," I warn him. "Don't leave a trail."

"My apologies."

We charge thirty feet into the tunnel before I call a halt. "Stand behind me. I'll take the hits; you two clean up."

Heart swivels on a dime and leaps behind the cover of my kite shield. Slayah backpedals and fires an arrow over my shoulder, knocking off a chunk of the nearest robot's health as its allies charge me.

I deflect the first robot's punch with my shield. Heart plunges her clockwork rapier into the robot's neck, scoring a critical hit that spatters us with oil. I finish the bot with a mace hit to the face.

Slayah's target throws me backward with a kick of its boxy foot. Exposed on the frontline, Heart slashes her blade across the wounded enemy's face and ends its digital life in a shower of red glass. The next enemy punches her in the chest, and a second robot kicks her for more damage.

"Down!" Slayah's bow zings. A glowing arrow lances through four robots clustered around Heart and stuns them long enough for her to recover.

Heart's saber glows red. She twirls like a ballerina, slashing every enemy around her multiple times. All four robots explode, and red glass falls on the dancing warrior like confetti.

"You guys." Heart cheers, "I unlocked a new Flair!"

"Excellent, Heart," says Slayah. "Based on Cryoblend's penchant for player synergy, our party may unlock group abilities as our skills and Affinity grow."

"Look out!" Another enemy looms behind her. I jump in and take its punch on my shield. Two strikes from my mace and another arrow glass it.

Just three robots remain, but Heart and I are both wounded. We cluster up with Slayah as the monsters attack. I'm too busy parrying to fight back.

"Slayah, Heart, cut them down!"

Heart leans around my shield and stabs one robot's steel-drum gut. Slayah shoots it dead.

Even outnumbered, the robots continue to pound on my shield. Heart circles around to their rear and leaves their glass remains littering the floor. Shouts and rapid footsteps from behind tarnish our victory.

"We have to move!" I urge the others. "Slayah, where are we?"

"I have a general idea, though these tunnels are unmapped. Finding a new path back to the main entrance will take time."

"No choice. The Hoods will catch us any second. Slayah, take point."

We dash through the darkness. Every time we encounter a mob of foes, we kite them to the next group around a random corner and kill them in a cluster. The Copper Hoods chase us the whole way. Their frustrated cries resonate down side tunnels, always one step behind. Their flickering torchlight draws nearer with every batch of foes we kill.

The clock in my party status screen strikes 5:00 a.m. We're all below 30 percent health. "Heart, you got any potions left?"

"Sorry, Chains. You used the last one half an hour ago."

"I know this passage." Slayah's normally static voice rises. "The next right will bring us back to the main tunnel. Then it is a straight shot to the front doors."

The Copper Hoods' shouts nip at our heels. The first of them rounds the corner and fires an arrow at us, narrowly missing Heart's head.

"Run," I shout, "just run for the front doors!"

The three of us hotfoot it down the main tunnel with arrows whizzing past us. Every few seconds, we pass into another monster cluster's territory and draw their attention. Soon we've got dozens of clattering, clanking foes on our tail. The Hoods stop shooting.

"Smart move," I gasp. "I wouldn't want to draw their attention, either."

Heart runs ahead of me. Her long legs eat up the cracked concrete, but Slayah outruns her. We all pay the cost in stamina. Slayah's the highest-level player here, and he's half out of steam.

The front door looms out of the shadows ahead. With a hundred monsters shaking the tunnel and ten Copper Hoods howling for blood, Slayah hits the front door.

It doesn't move.

Heart slams into his back. I wheel around and bring my shield up. "Slayah, get that door open!"

"It says I cannot open it while my party is being targeted!"

My stomach sinks to my boots. "Stay behind me. We'll find a way through this."

Slayah and Heart pile into the corner left of the door. I leap in front of them, and the first three skeletons smash against my raised shield. Their bony claws scrabble on its steel surface as their rusty blades probe for openings.

"Kill them," I shout.

Heart sweeps her clockwork rapier under my shield. Its reinforced blade cuts all three skeletons off at the knees. "They're weak versions from the front tunnel. Our upgraded weapons take them down fast."

I strain to keep the shield up as four more skeletons hurl themselves at it. "Yeah, but there's a hundred of these bastards. Keep killing!"

Slayah fires a stream of blue arrows. They streak through the enemy mobs, scattering robots and skeletons into red fragments. But the mobs keep coming. My health falls to 20 percent, then 15.

The Copper Hoods glare sullenly through the cresting waves of enemies. Their gleaming blades promise death if we survive the sea of monsters.

Heart keeps slashing under my shield as Slayah fires over it. The close confines amplify their labored breath. My health falls to 10 percent. We've killed half the monsters, but it's not enough.

I'm going to get my team killed.

I made the wrong call.

This is my fault.

Despair chews the edges of my soul.

I picture my father's face. The row of medals on our mantel. He never surrendered, even if it meant crawling through churned meat to rescue his allies.

My heart throbs, and with my next breath, red text scrawls across my vision.

Shields rank 300 achieved.

Athletics rank 300 achieved.

Affinity level 2 with HeartAtHome and Pu$$y_$layah_666 achieved.

What the hell does it mean?

I take a club to the face as I skim the message. My health drops to 7 percent.

Streaming viewer count has surpassed 100,000.

The thought of a hundred thousand people watching me fight for my life makes my skin crawl.

High-profile account powers granted: Combo Flairs unlocked.

Matching requisite skill ranks Acrobatics and One-handed Swords detected in HeartAtHome.

Matching requisite skill ranks in Archery and Perception detected in Pu$$y_$layah_666.

Combo Flair Siege Breaker now available.

Activate Siege Breaker with the following physical inputs.

Pressure builds in my hands and feet as the system tries to move them. I make the split-second decision to go with the pressure, throwing my arm wide despite the enemy horde. My swinging shield flares. Golden energy arcs outward in a battering wave, hurling robots and skeletons back from my desperate team.

Heart's rapier shimmers with golden light. Her arms twitch, but she fights the urge.

"Go with it," I shout at her.

Heart hurls herself forward. Her sword glows molten gold as she sweeps it back and forth. Each swing cleaves a handful of enemies in half. She cuts down twenty monsters and falls to one knee in a lake of red glass, panting for breath.

Golden light dawns behind me. Slayah nocks five arrows at once. He leaps over me, firing in midair. Five blazing arrows blow away four skeletons each. He lands on the ground and launches another volley.

The golden barrage glasses the remaining undead as the Copper Hoods stagger back, shielding their eyes and crying in terror.

The aggro tingle in my back subsides.

All Combo Flair entering cooldown, 30 minutes remaining.

"Get to the doors!" I hurl my shoulder against the giant oak portals. They burst wide open, spilling me into the cold light of dawn.

PerfectBlade stares down at me, his top hat shading his wide eyes. "Chains, what on earth—"

Slayah and Heart come boiling through the doors after me. They gape at the Knights of the Golden Dawn assembled on the dungeon's doorstep.

"Copper Hoods!" I grab my party and drag them deep into the allied formation. "They kidnapped Slayah, and they're coming to kill us."

Perfect stifles his surprise and barks orders. "Frontline, form up. Don't let a single Copper Hood come through those doors. Someone get our half-dead friends some healing potions."

SquirrelOfDeath shoves four healing potions into my hands. His smile crinkles his rich brown eyes. "I'm relieved you guys made it. Don't worry, we've got you."

"Thanks, Squirrel." I unstopper a potion but pause to make sure Heart and Slayah get theirs first. As their health bars climb back into safe territory, I gulp my potion down.

"Here come the Hoods," Rainpig shouts from the frontline.

The pursuing villains freeze before our small army. ChocolateReaper gnashes his teeth at me from behind his massed troops. "Chains, you coward! You call me out, then run to your mommy's skirts. Get your bitch ass over here, and lemme cut you."

"I'll take you on right now, you son of a bitch." I try to shove through the lines, but Perfect snatches my arm.

"No duels today, gentlemen. ChocolateReaper, I hear you abducted my left-hand man. You come near my people again, and I'll kill you."

Reaper spits on the ground. "Give me Chains and I'll leave."

"This is not up for debate." The authority in Perfect's voice stiffens my spine. Even the Hoods cower. Reaper and his cronies shove past us, glaring at me in sullen malice. The humiliated thugs traipse down the road toward town.

Perfect looks my party over. "You three good?"

"Yeah." I sigh. "Roughed up, but we made it."

"Glad to hear it. Squirrel, get these three some energy drinks. Chains, Slayah, Heart, fall in for the day's crawl."

"Whoa, buddy." I jab my finger at the open dungeon doors. "My party spent all day yesterday and all night fighting in there. We barely made it out. My fuel gauge is a mile past empty."

Perfect's eyes glint like ice. "We can't lose a whole day."

"Man," I argue, "one day isn't gonna—"

"Yes," Perfect chops the air with his hand. "One day *can* make all the difference." He turns to Slayah. "Map faster. Every day you delay, those Hoods will try to grab you again. You can rest when we've beaten the boss."

Heart opens her mouth, but Slayah cuts her off. "Understood, Perfect. Let us get to work."

Perfect smiles. "That's what I like to hear. Knights of the Golden Dawn, forward into the dungeon!"

CHAPTER 14

AN UNFORTUNATE REUNION

"Chains," Slayah pants one hour into our second dungeon crawl that day, "break left!"

"Got it." I duck aside. Slayah's arrow rockets over my shoulder to nail the robot before me right in its metal face. The enemy dies in a dazzling explosion.

"On your right, Chains." Heart ducks under my arm into the robot's vacant spot. She whirls like a ballerina on the red glass and cuts the bunched robots apart.

Three skeletons surge into the gaps.

"Got you, Heart." I leap in front of her with my shield raised. The skeletons' weapons scrape off. "Back me up."

"On it." Heart steps to my left side and stabs a skeleton through its red eye socket. I slam the others back. All three crumble to red glass that crunches underfoot as we march forward.

"Chains, Heart, hold on!" Perfect's voice cuts through the din of battle. "The rest of the frontline can't keep up."

In the excitement, Heart and I got a few yards ahead of the line. We hunker behind my shield and let the armored Knights catch up. Their charge mows down the surviving enemies. Red glass carpets the tunnel.

Rainpig glares at me from the other side of the formation. "Gotta show off, eh, Chains?"

"Teacher's pet," LaserToast spits.

"You guys are killing it today." Perfect claps me on the back with a cheery grin, a far cry from his ugly glare this morning when I asked for rest. I've chugged down a health potion and five energy drinks just to stay on my feet. Part of me wonders what the hell Cryoblend is injecting into my brain that keeps me awake every time I drink one.

I dip my head to our archer. "Rescuing Slayah forced us to work together." I consider telling him about the group Flair we unlocked, but a warning from my gut keeps my mouth shut.

"Keep it up. We've made record time today." Perfect raises his voice. "Slayah, how's that map coming?"

"Excellent progress, Perfect. We have mapped four new tunnels and appear to be zeroing in on a main line. Coupled with the data I gathered last night, I estimate we have doubled our daily speed regarding main passages. Of course, we have neglected twelve side tunnels—"

"Main passages are all that matter, Slayah. Keep up the speed. Every tunnel brings you closer to safety from the Copper Hoods."

"Understood."

Perfect spreads his smile around the crew. "Everyone take a lunch break. Catch a nap if you need one. I'm still fresh, so I'll scout ahead." He disappears into the darkness before us.

"He's sickeningly cheerful today." I plop down on the cement floor like a sack of rocks.

Heart settles nearby with a feminine groan. "How have we kept this up so long? I'd rather be on a chain gang."

Slayah strides over with his bow slung on his back. Dark circles surround his eyes. "Last night I made significant strides in skill ranks. I am approaching my optimal build."

"Archer?"

"Among other things. Do you have a build in mind?"

I mull it over. "I guess I'm going for defense. Protecting you jerks seems to be paying off. If I don't cover your asses, who will?"

Heart snorts. "Can't just say you enjoy being with us. Always with the bravado."

"Take away a man's bravado, and you leave him crying about his feelings. That ain't my style. What about you, Heart?"

"Pure offense. I want to clear this rotten game as fast as possible."

"Yeah? Your child's waiting for you at home, right?"

She hesitates. "My daughter. What about you two? Who's waiting for you at home?"

Slayah opens his mouth to answer but suddenly yanks his bow from his back. "Copper Hoods."

I lunge to my feet and peer down the tunnel. Three murky silhouettes rush past and disappear down a side tunnel.

"What do those bastards want?"

"Possibly to map the tunnels like us," says Slayah. "Or perhaps they seek fresh victims."

"Should we go grab Perfect?"

"We would only expose him. He scouts ahead every day, yet the Copper Hoods have never discovered him. Keep an eye on his health bar. We will act only if he appears to be in trouble."

I settle back down to the cold floor. "Sounds good. I need to grab some shut-eye."

"I'll do the same," Heart says. "I'm trashed."

"I shall keep watch for you," says Slayah.

I squint to force his espresso face into focus. "Aren't you tired?"

"Yes, but I am also used to going days without rest inside a virtual world."

"Weird, man. Wake me when Perfect gets back."

"Understood."

I drift off as soon as my head hits the ground.

• • • •

The ambush comes from nowhere.

"Help me, Chains!" Heart screams as she's engulfed by a whirring wave of robots.

"At least a hundred!" Slayah's voice cracks with desperation as he fires into the mob. "We need more defenders on the frontline."

"We just lost two more." Perfect surges to the frontline, slashing and stabbing, but he barely makes a dent in the clanking tide. "Chains, get to Heart."

I smash into the mob. Heart's clockwork blade glints just ahead of me through a cluster of foes. Red glass flies, but she disappears under the seething mob. The bots' fists rise and fall until green glass fountains into the air.

"Heart, no!" Fury overwhelms the despair storming through my brain. I hurl myself at the bots, but they press back twice as hard. Their flailing limbs separate me from the rest of the guild.

"Chains, help me!" Slayah screams as the bots fall upon him. His bow snaps in his hands as they crush him to the cement. I can only watch him die in a spray of green glass.

"You were supposed to save him!" Perfect's accusation stabs me in the heart. Robots press our leader on all sides. He parries their bludgeoning arms as his stamina plunges toward zero. "You were supposed to save us all, Chains."

Squirrel, Rainpig, LaserToast. The robots glass them all. My grief surprises me.

Perfect's stamina gives out, and he falls to one knee. The robots beat him to death.

It's just me against a tunnel full of robots. My friends' torches die and leave me in the dark.

The Dead Wall in Geartown looms large from the darkness. Dead players' carved names ooze blood that runs down the stone and soaks my boots. The name EnchantedBlizzard stabs my eye.

The names of three more I couldn't save appear below hers:

PerfectBlade
Pu$$y_$layah_666
HeartAtHome

My father's stern voice fills my ears. "I would have saved them. But you let them die. You couldn't even protect my daughter."

• • • •

"Chains! Chains, it's OK!"

Someone is screaming my name. A heavy weight presses on my chest, and enwrapping bonds smother me. I try to tear loose, but the restraints snap back around me.

"Chains, it's me, Heart. Stop screaming."

Her voice cuts through my terror. She's crushing my head against her soft breast. Slayah's lean arms enfold me, pinning my arms to my sides.

"What the hell, you guys?" I sputter.

"Chains? Oh, thank God." Heart loosens her grip and stares into my eyes. "You started screaming bloody murder. We couldn't wake you up."

Slayah releases me. I shove Heart off me and roll to my feet. "Just a bad dream."

Fear vies with concern in her expression. "One hell of a dream."

"It happens." I do my best to sound nonchalant, but my voice breaks.

Her concern wins. "Is this normal for you?"

Rainpig snorts like a fat hog, and LaserToast rolls around clutching his stomach. The rest of the guild pretends they didn't notice my freak-out.

Heart grabs my arm. I tug it away, but she holds tight. "Chains, do you—?"

"What the crap is going on over here?" Perfect comes storming from the darkness. "Who's screaming? I could hear it two tunnels away."

Rainpig catches his breath and jerks a thumb at me. "Sleeping beauty."

Perfect's coat creases as he folds his arms. "What the hell, Chains? You're giving away our position."

"Sorry." I can't meet his eye.

"Whatever," Perfect huffs dismissively. "Everyone on your feet. Time to—"

"No!" Heart's cry cuts across Perfect's orders. She swipes an invisible window shut, probably a text message. Panic contorts her face as her fingers dig into my arm. "My friends. They're in danger."

Her announcement cuts through my brain fog. "Where are they?"

"They're in a tunnel not far away. The Hoods dragged a group of enemies to ambush my friends."

The Dead Wall flits across my vision again. Blood weeps from the name EnchantedBlizzard.

What good are you? my father's ghost whispers.

Heart claws at my chest. "Chains, we need to go."

"We need to get back to mapping." Ice rimes Perfect's voice. "We can't interrupt our work for strangers."

I stare into Heart's eyes. "This time I won't let you down." I give Perfect a backward glance. "You guys map the tunnel ahead. We'll be right back."

Heart lights a torch, steps toward the side tunnel, and gestures pleadingly at me.

Perfect glares. "Fine. I'll keep scouting while you guys deal with your charity cases."

I move to join Heart. As I pass Perfect, his low hiss raises my hackles. "I'd end anyone else that interrupted my work, Chains. Make it fast."

I double-time it after Heart into the dark passage.

A message scrolls across my vision. **PerfectBlade has booted you from the party. Streaming viewer count: 0.**

Salty jerk. Hogging the limelight ain't enough. He's gotta boot us out of it.

"This way." Heart takes point as we wind deeper into the tunnels. We skirt a couple of enemy mobs and follow a trail of red glass on the cracked concrete.

"We must be getting close."

"They pinged my minimap just up ahead."

We turn right and enter a wide tunnel. A dropped torch illuminates two women battling a mix of forty robots and skeletons in a recessed center channel.

"Karma," Heart cries. "Mischief!" She slashes through the enemy ranks toward the small woman in clingy leather armor.

AznMischief backflips like an Olympian away from three slashing skeletons. She flicks her gloved hand at them in midair. Torchlight glints off a glass vial moments before the three skeletons blow apart in a blast that rattles the tunnel.

The muscly young woman at her back, MechaKarma, fires a rotary blunderbuss into the mob. Her coveralls fail to stabilize the ample bosom under her white blouse. Four robots disintegrate under the barrage.

A robot makes the mistake of closing with Karma while she's reloading. She gun butts its chrome-domed head, hurling it into the mob where it explodes into red glass.

Karma's cinnamon face splits in a grin. "Missy, I've killed eight so far! Isn't that awesome?"

Mischief flips away from a skeleton's blade. "Shut up and keep shooting!"

"Okaaaay!" Karma's blunderbuss roars, glassing a robot and a skeleton. Despite their heroic efforts, she and Mischief are still hopelessly outnumbered.

I shield bash through a cluster of robots and reach Heart. "Stay with me. Getting yourself killed won't help anyone."

"Then stop lecturing me and help *them*!"

I slide open my window and invite Heart, Mischief, and Karma into a party. Their health bars appear in my sidebar, and I gasp. "Holy crow, they're almost dead."

"Told you. Let's help out." Heart finishes two enemies wounded by Mischief's bomb and clears our way to her and Karma.

I cover the diminutive Mischief. "Heard you need help," I quip over the blows raining on my shield.

"My hero." Her sharp tone matches the dagger she hurls from cover. Two enemies crumble into glass. Another vial appears in her hand. She chucks it and engulfs four robots in a hissing acid cloud. Their steel skin corrodes away.

"Here." I shove a potion into her hand. She curls her fingers around it, and I get the message **Gift accepted.**

Mischief downs the potion with two dainty swallows. "I've got this side covered, stud. Go help that muscle-bound dairy cow over there."

Three paces away, a skeleton creeps up on the buxom gunner. I hit the undead with a running bash that scatters his red fragments into the melee.

Karma knocks on her woolly head with a grease-stained fist. "Thanks, Chains. Sometimes I forget to watch out."

"Uh, sure." I point to the robots converging on her back. "Look out!"

Karma turns and fires into the clanking mob. Her volley glasses two robots. She gives me a dopey grin. "Thanks again."

"Just drink this." I hand her my last potion. Her eyes sparkle like a kid in a candy store.

"Ooh, peaches. My favorite." She gulps it down in one go.

"Mischief," I shout, "Karma, get back against the tunnel wall."

"Whatever you say, stud."

"'Kaaaay."

"Heart, you and I take frontline and defend."

"Got it."

The four of us form two ranks. The last twenty monsters crash against us. Heart parries every blow directed at her as my shield clangs like a gong. Gun blasts and explosions tear into the semicircle of enemies.

Despite our tight formation, Heart takes several hits that drop her health to half. I move to shield her but get stabbed in the side and head. My pivot exposes Mischief, who takes a robot punch to the chest.

"Halfway there, guys," I pant. "Stay behind my shield and keep shredding them."

"I'd stay behind you if you'd quit moving," Mischief growls.

"Not much I can do when I've got three backliners to cover."

"The backline is boooring." Karma charges ahead, body-slamming two robots to the floor. She blows them away before they can rise.

Combo Flair unlocked.
Matching requisite skill ranks Acrobatics and One-handed Swords detected in HeartAtHome.
Combo Flair Meteor Rush now available.
Activate Meteor Rush with the following physical inputs.

"Heart."

"I saw it, too. Let's do it."

The system pressure builds in my left knee, so I drop down and raise my shield. It glows with golden light as Heart charges me, her right foot burning gold. She leaps and lands boot first on my shield. I follow the pressure and hurl her into the enemy. Her glowing blade carves a path of destruction through the last cluster of foes. Red glass splashes across the tunnel as she lands in a gymnast's dismount.

Heart gives me a thumbs-up. "We're learning new tricks by the handful."

I release a breath I didn't know I'd been holding. "That got hairy, but we made it. Karma, you're down to half health again."

"Yeah, I keep forgetting to buy better armor."

"Didn't I tell you before we left town?" Mischief reaches up and bops her much taller friend on the forehead.

Karma giggles. "I wanted to make sure you had time to buy your potion ingredients. And then you were so ready to go . . ."

Mischief facepalms. "Just say no if you're not ready, moron."

"Hey," I say, "go easy on her."

Mischief plants a hand on her slender hip. "She don't need your help. Neither do I."

"That why you sent me an SOS?"

"That was for Heart, not her boy toy." Mischief turns her back, drops from the party, and fiddles with some potions from her inventory.

"You're welcome." I turn and head into the darkness.

"Don't take her too serious, OK?" Karma whispers. "She's super grateful."

"Sure she is," I scoff. "You coming, Heart?"

Heart gives Mischief a quick hug. "It was good to see you again." She goes to hug Karma, but the big girl crushes her in a bear hug that gives me sympathy pains.

Heart staggers over to me. "I'm coming. Know where we're going?"

The dank maze stretches before me. "To be honest, I got turned around. I'd ping Slayah, but we're not in a party. Even Karma left."

"If I remember Slayah's map, hugging the left wall should get us back to the main tunnel."

"Sounds good to me." I take the lead while Heart lights the way. We keep left, but the slimy tunnels all look alike. Finally, we turn a corner and find a pile of red glass.

"Someone's been here recently," Heart says softly.

"Our backtrail should have filled in already."

"Must be someone else."

"Yeah, but friendlies or hostiles?"

We follow the red trail to a confluence of tunnels, where Heart grabs my arm. "I hear voices."

"So do I. Kill the light."

She extinguishes her torch, plunging us into darkness. The sound of whispering grows louder as we creep down the tunnel in the pitch black. I stow my weapon to give myself a free hand just in case. After another thirty feet, I make out ten figures gathered in the light of a small lantern, but they're too far away for their name tags to appear.

"I know I screwed up. But the bastards took him right out of our hands."

Heart stifles a gasp. "That's ChocolateReaper."

I clench my fists. Reaper stands in a circle of Hoods, talking to someone in a black robe with a copper cowl.

The robed figure slashes the air with one hand. His voice is a death-metal growl, like he's talking deeper than normal. "Not my problem. That archer was your ticket. You failed."

Heart's breath tickles my ear. "Hey Chains, doesn't that guy's voice sound sorta familiar?"

"Maybe, but I can't place it."

"It's that asshole, Chains." Reaper snarls my name. "He screwed up the plan."

"No excuses," Captain Vocal Fry snaps. "I expect results. If you can't furnish them, I'll find someone who can."

"Not necessary," Reaper insists. "I'll kill Chains and his bitch next time."

"Patience," the robed man croaks. "Chains has almost outlived his usefulness. When he does, you can do as you please with him and the woman. Understand?"

Reaper gives an animal growl. "Yes."

"Yes, what?"

"Yes . . . sir."

The robed man sweeps a gloved hand across the surrounding tunnel mouths. "Now, go do your jobs." The meeting breaks up as Copper Hoods head in every direction. Reaper and three goons stalk down a side tunnel as the cloaked leader picks up his lantern and slips down the main passage.

"Follow him," I whisper.

His head jerks toward us.

My ear barely registers Heart's voice. "I think he heard you."

The leader stands frozen. When Heart and I don't make another sound, he hurries down the tunnel.

We sneak after him as quickly as we dare. I yearn to get close enough to see his nameplate, but I've neglected my Stealth skill in our mad rush to conquer the dungeon. Heart and I tail him at the edge of visibility as he scurries through the dark.

"Wait, I know this area," Heart murmurs. "We should be close to camp."

"Why would the Copper Hood leader . . .?" Light from multiple torches spills into the tunnel through a high arch ahead. The leader stops beside the entrance to camp, unequips his cloak, and stashes his lantern.

Heart gasps aloud.

His disguise gone, PerfectBlade turns his clean-cut face to stare right at us.

CHAPTER 15

THIS TERRIBLE GLASS

"**B**astard!" I run at Perfect and throw a punch. He ducks under my fist. "You miserable sack of crap. I trusted you!"

"What's all this noise?" Two Knights hustle through the arch, carrying torches. Light spills over Perfect, Heart, and me as my shield's edge misses Perfect's head and sparks on the wall.

The two guards pull their weapons. "Chains, why are you attacking Perfect?"

"He's gone mental!" Perfect's voice expertly balances panic and contempt.

I jab a finger at the turncoat. "Perfect has been meeting with the Copper Hoods every time he sneaks off. He's their leader."

Everyone in camp crowds around the arch. The Knights' ranks have grown since Heart and I joined. Eighteen pairs of eyes shift between Perfect's composed face and my quivering scowl.

"It's true." Heart steps in front of me. "Perfect told them they can kill us when he's done with us."

"You're both sick." Perfect shakes his head and slithers back into the Knights' armed ranks.

Only Slayah regards Perfect with calculating scrutiny.

I jab my finger at the top-hatted snake hiding behind our guildmates. "Check his inventory. He's got a cloak with a copper hood."

"How are we supposed to check that?" SquirrelOfDeath asks. "Player inventories are private."

I grind my teeth. "I tell you, it's in there."

"Here's what's in my inventory." Perfect manifests a little square of parchment and waves it aloft. "I've got a map of the surrounding side tunnels. Doesn't this prove I've been scouting?"

I don't miss a beat. "You got that map from your Copper Hood buddies."

"Sure, Chains," Perfect scoffs. "The Hoods are my buddies. I've only risked my life saving you from them three times."

"It's not risking your life if you hold their leash, asshole."

Perfect clicks his tongue. "Typical manipulator. Lots of insults and zero facts." He draws every eye as he spreads his arms wide. "Isn't it a fact that I saved each of you from those sociopaths?"

Seventeen Knights murmur assent. Only Slayah remains silent.

"The Copper Hoods are murderers," Perfect thunders. "Whom have I killed?"

Heart shakes her fist. "You killed my friends!"

Perfect gives her a condescending look. "Where's my name on the Dead Wall?

"Just because you didn't hold the sword doesn't mean you don't have blood on your hands."

As Heart argues, Rainpig and LaserToast slip into the shadows to my left. I pretend not to notice.

"I see what this is." Perfect snaps his fingers. "You're jealous of me, right, Chains?"

"What the hell are you talking about?" I sputter.

Perfect turns in a slow circle. "You want everyone here to think you're as big a hero as I am. I should have known your guilt would give you a hero complex."

The concrete under my boots seems to become quicksand. "My what?"

"Your guilt." Fake pity tinges Perfect's glare. "You confessed it to me yourself. I'm not the killer, Chains. You are!"

"That's complete bullshit!" I almost pull my blade and go for Perfect right there. But fifteen armored troops stand between us, and they're pointing their weapons at me.

Perfect smirks at me over their heads. "You fabricated a story to discredit me in front of the guild. What kind of lowlife backstabs his benefactor, Chains?"

"That's a lie." Heart turns her pleading gaze on the armed men shuffling to enclose us. "I saw him, too."

Slayah slips around the crowd to our right.

"Poor girl," Perfect purrs. "Chains's hero act fooled you. But all is forgiven. Just come back to us."

"Never," Heart growls. "I know the truth."

Perfect's eyes glint with joy. "What a pity."

I lean close to Heart and whisper, "Stop. We both know his secret. Nobody else will if we don't get out of here alive."

Heart reluctantly stands down. I lead her away from the encroaching Knights.

"How much are they paying you?" Perfect calls out.

My brain can't process his question. "What?"

"How much are the Copper Hoods paying you to frame me?"

"Get real, asshole. I would never work with those monsters." It's all the defense I can muster.

Perfect shakes his head. "It's a betrayal as old as Julius Caesar. The Copper Hoods conspire with my close ally to destroy the only real threat to their power."

"You don't seriously believe this crap, do you?" I scan the Knights encircling Heart and me. All their expressions look cold and sullen.

"At last, we cut to the heart of it." Perfect's orator's voice rebounds from the concrete walls. "Chains and Heart are Copper Hood agents.

Their story of going to help their friends was a smokescreen for a meeting with Reaper's thugs. They chanced upon me on the way back and planned a hasty ambush."

"You bastard," Heart seethes. "Chains warned *you* about Copper Hoods on your trail."

Perfect steamrolls Heart. "But their clumsiness alerted the camp, so they concocted another lie to cover the first. It's so devious, it might have worked had they not been so impulsive." He sniffs with unbearable sanctimony. "Chains, you sicken me."

Anger rips away my filter. "You're batshit crazy if you think everybody wants to kiss your ass."

"Let's ask the people who know you best. Knights of the Golden Dawn, whom do you believe? Me, the man who saved your lives and gave you a place to belong? Or Chains, the admitted killer who keeps you all at arm's length?"

The Knights' eyes grow colder. Even SquirrelOfDeath glowers at me.

Perfect's lips spread over his too-white teeth. "Weren't all of you assaulted on your first day?"

Fifteen voices answer in chorus: "Yes."

"And didn't I step in and save you all?"

"Yes."

"Didn't I take you in, protect you, and give you a home?"

"Yes."

The Knights' litany freaks me out. But their leader's words finally penetrate my brain. "Has that been your game all along, Perfect? Set up a brute squad to victimize people, then ride in as the hero? Is that how you snatch up the best talent for your guild?"

Surprise tarnishes Perfect's golden smile.

A grim laugh escapes my chest. "I nailed it, huh?"

Perfect snarls. "I'm not a villain like you. I've cared for this guild. I've protected them. What have you done but alienate them? You've grown faster than anyone else here and kept your methods to yourself, while I train them to get stronger as a unit. You're a nobody, Chains. Just a double agent trying to blame your betters."

"Betters?" I draw myself up. "That's the difference between us. I know I'm as screwed up as the next guy."

"Clearly," Perfect snaps. "Let's put it to a vote. Who do you all believe: the man who rescued you or the asshole who barely speaks to you and almost gave away our position?"

Ten feet to my left, Rainpig and LaserToast share hyena grins.

"Chains betrayed us!" Rainpig squeals.

"Justice for the victims!" bleats LaserToast.

Pigman chops at my legs while Toast swings at my head. I block Rainpig's blow and duck under LaserToast's slash. The two of them flank me. Heart steps in to parry Pig's thrust as I block Toast's slash, but the other fifteen Knights close in.

Slayah leaps between me and the closing mob. "Please, wait. This is madness. We cannot just—"

Rainpig points his sword at Slayah. "The android's with them. Stick him, too."

The mob surrounds Slayah, Heart, and me. Perfect only frowns as his guild turns on its three most effective members.

Slayah presses his back to mine and draws his bow. "How can this be happening?"

"You really were sheltered." I block another of LaserToast's strikes.

Heart's sword clashes with Pigman's axes. "What do we do, Chains? We're outnumbered."

"We fight our way out." My shield catches Toast's blade. I kick him in the gut and send him toppling back into the mob.

Chaos descends. Sword and spear and axe cut the air and batter through armor. My party's health bars creep lower with every blow.

Beyond the kill circle, Perfect stands with his unsullied blades at the ready and his eyes fixed on me.

In the midst of absolute madness, SquirrelOfDeath raises his spear for a thrust at Heart's back. Another spearhead stabs from Enchanted's chest and into my mind. I remember her screaming and clawing at the iron spike between her breasts. I remember the crystal chime of her body shattering into green glass.

SquirrelOfDeath's health bar is almost empty. So is Heart's. My shield is holding back Toast's sword. My saber lacks the leverage to parry Squirrel's two-handed thrust.

I stab Squirrel in the head. His health bar drops to zero. He turns to me with shock written on his face before it ruptures into a cloud of green glass.

The rest of the mob freezes. Even Rainpig and LaserToast stiffen with surprise at the first death.

"You killed him." Perfect's soft tone stabs me in the heart. "You murdered Squirrel."

I jab my blade toward Perfect. "You set us against each other."

"Don't blame me, Chains. Squirrel's name is on the monument with you as his murderer. Now everyone knows the truth about you."

My eye darts to a message in the corner of my vision.

Streaming Viewer Count: 150,000.

My former allies glare at me with bared teeth and pinprick pupils. They advance again.

"Slayah, Heart. Use our group combo."

"That may kill them," Slayah warns me.

I step closer to him and Heart. "If we don't, they'll kill us."

Slayah reaches for his quiver. "Understood."

Heart's voice wavers, but she readies her sword. "I trust you, Chains."

I raise my shield.

Combo Flair Siege Breaker selected. Follow the guided motions
to activate.

Golden light envelops my kite shield. I swing my shield arm, and an energy wave forces the Knights back twenty feet.

Heart's saber shimmers like gold as she hurls herself forward. Her blade leaves afterimages as she scythes into the front ranks and drives them to their knees.

Slayah leaps over my head and fires five arrows into the crowd. He lands and shoots another golden volley. All ten missiles punch into the concrete at the massed Knights' feet and detonate like dazzle grenades. Our attackers shriek and cover their eyes.

"Run!" I shove Heart and Slayah ahead of me down the tunnel and take my own advice.

A wailing chorus sounds behind us.

"Which way did they go?"

"I can't see!"

Perfect's voice bounces off the walls as we run. "Everyone will see Squirrel's name on the monument alongside his murderer's. You hear me, Chains? You're marked!"

My blood runs cold.

Slayah, Heart, and I flee through the dark tunnel toward the front doors.

CHAPTER 16

DECISIONS

We tumble out of the tall dungeon doors and into the sunlight. Heart, Slayah, and I run to the nearby woods. Hidden among the trees, we collapse onto a crisp bed of dry leaves.

"I just killed someone," I moan. "Again. I did it again!"

Heart's voice cracks. "It's not your fault, Chains. You saved my life."

"She is correct, Chains," says Slayah.

"Easy for you guys to say. You didn't just look a man in the eye and glass him."

"It would have been Heart, if not him." Slayah stands and brushes dead leaves off his pants. "What is our next move?"

"You two need to get the hell away from me. Perfect was right. I'm a marked man."

Heart's auburn mane whips as she shakes her head. "I won't leave you."

"I'm an outcast now, sweetheart." I climb to my feet and turn my back. "And Perfect's out for my head. Guess I'm no more use to him."

"It is likely he has also marked Heart and me for death," says Slayah. "And the Copper Hoods also have ample reason to despise us."

"Slayah's right, Chains. The Copper Hoods hate us just as much as they hate you. Perfect and his guild are hunting us, too. Without you, we're done for."

I punch a tree. It feels good to vent my anger, so I smack my fist against the ridged bark a few more times. "Why did you join us, Slayah? You could have stayed silent."

"No, I could not. Too many data points added up. Besides, you have been tremendously kind to me. And Heart has shared her delicious cooking."

"It really is the way to a man's heart," the chef in question boasts.

"I employ pure logic," Slayah insists.

I give him a skeptical look. "Pure logic, huh?"

"Mostly. Also, you are my friend. I could not watch them slaughter you."

His admission touches my heart. I clear my throat to avoid getting choked up. "Thanks, Slayah. You're my friend, too."

Heart rests her slender hand on his shoulder. "And mine. You're *both* weird, but I trust the two of you more than anyone else in this digital prison."

"I trust you guys, too." A second after I say the words, it dawns on me that they're true.

Heart bows her head. "I know it hurts to have killed someone, Chains. I've . . . felt that guilt before. And I'm not gonna leave when you need a friend more than ever."

"Nor will I, Chains. Your name on the Dead Wall means you will need assistance navigating a hostile society. I intend to stand beside you and help however you will allow."

"You guys are nuts. You really should cut and run. Anyone else would."

"Sure. But who wants to be normal?" Slayah gives my ear a small smile.

"Slayah, look me in the eye."

His dark eyes widen, but he meets my gaze. "Why?"

"It's a sign of respect. Your father never taught you to look a man in the eye when you speak?"

"My father was not present. My guardian did not explain this social dynamic."

"Well, I'm telling you now. Always look people in the eye when you talk."

"Strange. But understood. I will do that from now on, Chains."

"Rounding out your rough edges is gonna be a group project," says Heart.

I sigh. "If you two insist on sticking with a marked killer, our first group project is gonna be figuring out how to stay alive."

Slayah embraces me. I'm still reeling from the surprise when Heart joins the group hug.

I manage to disentangle myself. "All right, you sappy goofs. The two biggest prison gangs are hunting us, we didn't sleep last night, and I'm hungry enough to eat a skunk's asshole. Let's head back to town before word gets out."

They both beam at me. We march through the woods toward town. Their tromping footsteps cover my whisper.

"I killed again, Dad. One more disappointment."

CHAPTER 17

OUTLAWS

W e're halfway down the cobblestone road to the inn when Slayah stops me.

"Hey," I groan. "What gives? I'm tired."

"Quiet." Slayah shoves me into an alley. Heart squawks as he throws her in. He dives after us.

I straighten my shirt. "Why'd you do that?"

"I saw ChocolateReaper by the inn." Slayah creeps to the alley's mouth, peeks around the corner, and ducks back. "Yes, it is him. He and five other armed men are lurking in the alley next to the front door. They are not wearing their hoods, but I recognize them from my capture."

"How did they get on our trail so fast?" Heart ponders aloud.

"Perfect must have sent word it's open season on us," I growl. "I'll gut that bastard."

Heart looks stricken. "What are we gonna do?"

"We'll have to lay low for a while. You guys know any other inns off the main drag?"

"I do," says Heart, "but everyone there will recognize your name. If Perfect has the Copper Hoods looking for you . . ."

Her logic slaps me in the face. "Then I'm not safe anywhere. None of us are. The whole damn city's a death trap."

Slayah ushers us out the back of the alley. "We will sleep in the wild."

"In the wild?" Heart looks scandalized. "With the monsters?"

"He's right, Heart. Either we take our chances outside the city, or we find some deserted alley to hole up in."

"The alleys don't have skeletons," Heart argues.

"No," I admit, "but Geartown's full of killers stalking the streets for victims after dark. At least the computer monsters are predictable."

Heart deflates. "OK. But let me stop somewhere and get us some dinner."

"Better get rations for tomorrow, too," I advise. "We'll have to avoid the city until things cool down."

The three of us wind through back roads toward Geartown's exit. Heart grabs us dinner at some burger joint while Slayah buys rations at the general adventuring store. I hide in a reeking alley.

We wait until dusk, slip through the gates, and head into the wild. A few players pass us on their way back to town. They give me a wide berth.

"Looks like word is already spreading." Heart gives me a sad glance.

"I'm not used to being liked anyway. Hatred is just business as usual."

"I experience much the same," says Slayah.

Heart sighs. "Great. I'm exiled with two professional pariahs."

"Yes, but where precisely are we exiled *to*?"

"Monsters are pretty sparse in the woods near here," says Heart. "It's where all the female players harvest herbs."

We follow her, serenaded by chirping crickets, to the forest. True to Heart's word, the giant fuzzy caterpillars that lair here are spaced so widely that we easily find a campsite outside their territory.

We wolf down our burgers. The food tastes like ash in my mouth, but it fills the hole in my belly. Slayah manifests three thick blankets and hands them out.

Heart slaps her forehead. "I didn't think to buy camping equipment. Thanks, Slayah."

"You are welcome." He lies down in the hollow between two roots and falls asleep in moments.

Heart settles down with her back against a tree. "He was probably even more exhausted than us."

"Being kidnapped is hard work."

"I'll take first watch, Chains. You get some sleep."

"You're just as tired as I am."

"I'm used to sleep deprivation. I'm a mother, remember? Besides, I've seen you drooping every time you think we aren't looking."

"I'm gonna buy one of those helmets that encloses my whole face."

"It's fine, Chains." Her voice is soft and her eyes softer. "You don't have to hide it from me. I know it hurts."

"What do you know? I've killed two people now."

"Well, I—"

"The last thing I need is someone trying to get close to me. You want first watch? Cool. Wake me up in a few hours." I roll over in my blanket, feeling like a jerk for lashing out at her. But she got too damn close.

It feels like I'll never sleep on the bumpy ground, but exhaustion takes its toll. The dark forest and the ambient cricket noises soothe me. I fall asleep within minutes.

• • • •

It's a long night of troubled dreams. Mostly fighting monsters in an endless tunnel. The tunnel turns into a dark hallway with a lit doorway at the far end. A woman screams on the other side. When I shove open the door, Squirrel jumps at me with blood running down his wide face. My sword is stuck through his skull. "It hurts, Chains," he cries. "Make it stop!"

• • • •

I wake screaming in the dark forest. Someone is squeezing me. I try to fight, but Heart's voice crashes through my terror.

"It's OK, Chains. It's all right. You're safe."

I shove her aside and roll onto my belly. I need to vomit, but the game system doesn't let me, so I dry heave into the soil until the nausea passes. Heart rubs my back the whole time.

"I know you don't want to talk about it, but maybe you'll feel better if you do."

"Nothing's gonna make me feel better, Heart. I killed Squirrel. I have to live with that. Just like I have to live with killing my neighbor."

Heart stops rubbing. "What do you mean?"

"I beat him to death. That's why I'm in here."

"Why?"

The words won't come out. They're eating me alive on the inside, but I haven't said them to anyone. Even at my trial, I refused to testify.

I suck in a breath to steady my nerves. "I found him raping my sister."

Heart lays a hand on my back again and caresses it. My mother was the last one to soothe me like that, the day my dad died.

"Oh, Chains. I'm so sorry."

"Feel sorry for her. I'm not the one it happened to."

"You love her, right?"

"With all my heart."

"Then you share her pain. He hurt her. But he hurt you, too. Otherwise you would have walked away. Instead, you killed him."

"You don't get it, though. My dad was a Reclaimer in the war."

"Wow, that *is* impressive."

"He left Mom and Sis in my protection. It was my job to keep them safe. And I failed. Then I killed the guy. Now I'm in here. They paid rent with my paycheck. I killed a man and left my family helpless."

"Chains, you can't judge yourself like that."

"My dad was a war hero, Heart. He crawled across battlefields to rescue the wounded. I couldn't even keep his daughter safe."

"You're his son. I'm sure he forgives you."

I cradle my throbbing head. "I can't get that image of my sister out of my brain. I see her naked and bloody every time I close my eyes. It's stuck in there like a splinter in my eye."

"I'm so sorry, Chains."

"I don't need sympathy. I'm stuck playing a video game while my sister and mother are out there alone. How are they eating? Are they homeless? The last time I saw them was at my sentencing. My sister looked like death warmed over. She hates me now. They both must hate me."

"They don't hate you. No mother could hate her child."

I shove her hand away and roll over in the darkness to sit against a tree. "How the hell do you know what I'm feeling, Heart? I've killed two men. And I don't even have the luxury of regret, because I killed them both to help someone I care about. I just keep on killing and failing. How would you know what that's like?"

Heart sits quiet for a while. The silence stretches on so long I don't think she's gonna answer. Then, in a small voice:

"I killed them."

"What?"

"I shot and killed three intruders who murdered my husband."

Now it's my turn to be silent.

"They broke in. My husband took his unregistered pistol and went to check out the noise. They shot him dead in the hallway. I was sleeping in my daughter's room. She's two years old. His pistol came flying in the door. I scooped it up and shot them when they gathered around his body. A civilian using a gun is worse than murder in the People's Republic of California. Now I'm in prison for twenty years. Even if I survive this game, my daughter won't remember me."

"Damn. I'm really sorry."

Heart shrugs. "That's how it goes. We both have our reasons, right?"

"I guess so. And I'm sorry about your husband."

She's quiet for another beat. "Thanks."

Before I can question her halfhearted response, she takes a deep breath.

"The point is, facing death to get home and help your family honors your father's memory."

"Thanks, but I know I let my father down. I also know he'd fight to keep Perfect's cult from taking over and terrorizing the weaker players. My dad's not here, so Geartown will have to settle for me."

Heart smiles at me. "They'll have to settle for both of us."

I give her a half smile in return. "Remember what you're getting into. Perfect has a fanatical cult and a dungeon map. Clearing the boss before them will take a miracle."

"Hey, we made it this far. I'm sticking with you."

"Your funeral. Go ahead and pass out. I'll take second watch now."

"Good night, Chains. And thanks for the honesty."

"Don't mention it. *Ever.*"

"It'll be our secret." Heart wraps up in her blanket and falls asleep.

I sit wide awake with my memories as the digital crickets chirp their melody.

CHAPTER 18

THREE'S COMPANY, FIVE'S A PARTY

"Sleeping outside is not as bad as I feared." Slayah rolls up his blanket in the cold, clear dawn and stows it in his inventory. Nearby, Heart rises much more slowly. Her bleary eyes scan the clearing until they lock onto me.

I wave. "Morning."

"Hmm." Her eyes drift shut. She's fallen asleep sitting up.

"Heart, we gotta get into town before the gangs wake up."

"Zzzzzz . . ."

"Heart, skeletons!"

"Where?" She leaps to her feet and spins like a dervish. I can't contain a guffaw.

Heart glares at me through the auburn hair that's fallen over her eyes. "Stop laughing."

I choke back my laughter. "Your face was priceless."

Her sluggish kick barely scuffs my left greave. "Jerk."

Slayah blinks at me. "Heart has a valid question. Where are the skeletons?"

I smooth things over with Heart and Slayah. We stuff our blankets back into our inventories and leave the forest.

"Six o'clock on the dot," I read from my status window. "We'll have the town to ourselves."

My view of the field in front of Slayah shimmers as he opens his window and swipes through menus. "It would be best to convert our drops into cash, then stock up on durable rations and drinks. Do we intend to sleep in town any time soon?"

I hold up my right palm. "Perfect and the Copper Hoods want our heads." I hold up my left. "Then again, they're more concerned with clearing the boss than killing us. Let's play it by ear."

Slayah shakes his head. "Perfect has demonstrated vindictive behavior in the past. I think it unlikely he will simply forget us."

"If he comes in force, we three don't stand much chance."

Heart speaks up as we approach the city gates. "I've been thinking about that. Let me check out some leads."

I frown at her. "On your own?"

"Most of the people who'd attack us are still asleep. How about we split up, get our tasks done, and meet back in the center plaza at seven?"

"Good plan. See ya then, Heart."

She scurries off through the deserted streets.

I turn to Slayah. "Got anything pressing?"

"Not particularly. I travel with my possessions, so I do not need to return to my lodgings."

"Same here. Let's dump our loot for cash."

"The nearby player-owned loot shop should be open. They will likely provide the best pay per item."

"Lead on, bro."

I follow Slayah down a couple of winding streets. A few players drift out of their pipe-riddled houses. They give me a wide berth. One older woman glares death beams at me.

"Looks like word's spreading."

Slayah enters a garish blue shop. The hanging sign above the door depicts a dead goblin with all four limbs stuck in the air.

"Good morning, shopkeep."

"Oh, Slayah. Bright and early as always. What—?" The bald shop-keeper jumps so hard his belly wobbles. He jabs a sausage finger at me. "What're you doin' with *him*?"

"We are party members. I told him you provide the best pay."

"Not to murderers I don't. Get out." He throws a bottle at us. It breaks at my feet. "Out of my shop, weirdos, and don't come back!"

We trudge back into the street.

"I certainly did not expect that response."

"Don't take it personal, man. My name is mud."

"I thought your name was Chains."

"Get out of here!" The old lady who gave me the evil eye shoos me away like a stray dog. "We don't want your kind on our street."

"OK, granny. Keep your top on. For all our sakes."

Slayah and I head down the street as the old bat shrieks curses after us.

"Guess we're dropping our goods at the NPC general store."

Of all the places in town, the general store is the only one full of people. I get dirty looks as soon as I enter.

"It's the murderer."

"I heard he killed a player in cold blood."

"Walking around town like he owns the place."

Even Slayah draws up short. "It appears you are recognized here."

"Word's spreading too fast. I smell a rat, Slayah. A rat with a Napoleon complex."

I slink through the crowds to the NPC vendor along the back wall. Four tough guys in leather armor cut me off when I step inside. "Where you goin', killer?"

"Just dropping some loot. I'll be outta here in a minute."

"You'll be outta here *now*."

I try to hold back. But my mouth has always run like a greyhound. "I'm trying to earn a living, asshole. I'll be done quicker than your mom's customers."

The whole room turns to stare. Someone spits at my feet.

The biggest tough guy takes a step forward. "Out. Or you're leaving in pieces."

I scan the room. Not one friendly face in the bunch. I shake my head and leave.

Slayah trots along beside me. "This could prove troublesome. We need cash to purchase supplies. I could take your goods in for you."

"Won't work. They just saw you with me. Let them cool off, and we'll try back later. Maybe the equipment shops won't be as full."

The armor shop only holds a couple of schoolgirls who're probably in for turning tricks without a license. They scurry out with nervous glances as Slayah and I visit the counter.

"Good morning, travelers," the busty redhead owner greets us from behind the counter. "Looking to fortify your defense?"

"You should qualify for upgraded armor," Slayah says.

"I ain't even checked my stats since we foiled your kidnapping. Wonder how I'm doing."

BrokenChains
Level 62

"Holy crappin' lizards. I guess we did kill a mountain of enemies. What are my best skill ranks now?"

Acrobatics 300
Athletics 500
Brawling 570
Heavy Armor 570
Intimidate 450
Maces 450
One-handed Swords 570
Perception 600
Shields 600

I goggle at the numbers for a second. "Slayah, we damn near doubled my stats overnight."

"As you said, we faced a tremendous challenge. Thirty-six hours of nearly continuous combat pays ample returns."

"I scooped up some cash from a few of the kills. It should cover an armor upgrade." I tap the counter. "Looks like Heavy Armor 500 unlocked Scale Mail."

> Flimsy Scale Mail Shirt purchased.
> Flimsy Scale Mail Pants purchased.
> Flimsy Scale Mail Greaves purchased.
> Flimsy Scale Mail Gauntlets purchased.
> Goblin Hide Leather Belt purchased.
> Steel Kite Shield upgraded to rank 4.

The new scaly armor clinks when I walk. "Sounds like coins. Even the flimsy scale stuff is better than my steel chain mail set. Weird ranking system."

Slayah shakes his head. "Think about it. Right now, the level cap on this server is nine hundred ninety-nine. And we are still working on the first of fifty steps. The developers need a system to scale up the gear as we advance."

"Guess so. Feels crappy to upgrade to something designated as *flimsy*, though."

"You could simply upgrade the armor you have."

"Nah, I'd rather jump to the new category. I'll make more noise when I walk, but the base armor rating is much higher. Let's go next door and upgrade our weapons, then grab some potions."

The NPC weapon and item shops are just as devoid of customers. I walk away with a rank 4 steel shield, a matching mace, ten health potions, and five antidotes.

Slayah pockets his own potions as we leave. "You intend to use two shields, Chains?"

"I'll switch back and forth between a weapon and double shields. The skeletons resist sword damage, so I figure it's best to go with my strengths. You picking up anything but the bow?"

"My bow includes a melee upgrade. The top point is a spear blade. The bottom has a weight, like a mace." He turns the bow to show me. "I prioritize range, but I can survive if enemies slip through the frontline."

"They won't. I'll keep you safe, so you can focus on sniping. Just don't shoot me in the back."

"I will try to avoid it." His tone is dry as a desert, but his mouth quirks just enough to tell me he's joking.

We head back to the town square. A few working girls in dental floss dresses do the morning walk of shame back to whatever hole they call home. Even they stop to spit at me.

I check my status window again. "It's five to seven. Hope the pitchforks and torches hold off till then."

"If it is any comfort, I suspect the crowds will stop short of killing you. There is little distinction between killers and killers of killers. Few would wish to join you in infamy."

"Blood gets hot, Slayah. Not everyone is as logical as you are."

"With that statement, I agree."

Heart comes running up. Karma and Mischief tag along behind her. Karma droops her head with a sheepish smile, while Mischief regards me like a skunk carcass.

"This is your up-and-coming party, Heart?" Mischief crosses her leather-clad arms. "Not a chance. No offense, stud, but even the gentle sociopaths of Geartown can't scrape you off their shoes fast enough."

"Fine by me, princess. The party interface only gives us five slots until we open a guild, so we don't have room for both you *and* your attitude."

"Both of you, please." Heart casts pleading looks between us. "Chains, starting our own guild is the only way to get a house and stop sleeping outside. We need every ally we can get. Mischief is dependable, and she's shrewd."

Mischief sticks out her flat chest.

"That may be true," I say, "but her smug rating is off the charts."

"And you." Heart rounds on the little scoundrel. "Chains saved your life twice. No matter what the rest of the server says, you've seen his character for yourself."

Mischief deflates a little. "Yeah, but—"

"But you'll be an outcast if you join us," Heart interrupts. "Aren't you already?"

Mischief looks away.

Despite being the tallest and most curvaceous of the three women, Karma's voice is tiny as she rubs her hands nervously. "Heart's right, Missy. You always tell me we can't trust anyone. That we have to go it alone. Wouldn't it be nice to have friends?"

Mischief shoots Karma a withering glare. "Signing with this crew will *guarantee* we'll never have any friends."

Heart sighs. "People have already seen you two with me. Perfect will find out you're my friends. He leads the Golden Dawn and the Copper Hoods."

Mischief's eyebrows jump off her forehead. "No shit?"

"It's true." My fists clench at the memory. "He blackballed us because we caught him giving orders to his stooge, ChocolateReaper."

"What a fix." Mischief blows a stray lock of black hair off her forehead. "Breakin' my balls here, Heart."

"I'm sorry."

Mischief raises a gloved hand. "'S OK. This mushy cow and I were already on the copper tops' hit list. Getting to be so a pretty girl can't walk Geartown without an army." She sizes me up. "When you saved us, were you just showing off for Heart, or are you for real?"

"Define 'for real.'"

"Are you a good man?"

"No. But I'm trying."

Mischief shrugs. "At least you're honest."

"He's got a personal reason to get home," Heart says apologetically. "As good a reason as you and I have."

Mischief's mouth forms into a hard line. Her shoulders slump, and she sighs. "Fine. If you trust him, Heart, I will, too. God knows how bad I need to get home, and I can't be choosy. Sign us up."

I look at Karma. "You, too?"

She smiles big and warm. "Yuppers. Where Missy goes, I go."

Mischief points at Slayah. "What about the satanic cat-killer?"

Heart clears her throat. "Despite his display name, he's the smartest man in this game. Promise. We can't get out of here without him."

Slayah scratches his head. "What is wrong with my name? I was told that women find sexual prowess attractive in a mate."

Mischief raises an eyebrow at him. "There's confident swagger, then there's spray painting 'Sex Machine' on the side of your windowless van. You're squarely in van territory."

"I cannot believe the internet lied to me."

Mischief pinches the bridge of her nose. "You crazy bastards really do need me, don't you?"

Heart takes her hand. "Yes, we do."

I slide open my party window and send the two recruits invites and friend requests. Mischief and Karma accept both. "Every little bit helps," I think out loud.

Mischief's mouth puckers. "Helps with what?"

"Clearing the first dungeon before the Golden Dawn and the Copper Hoods," blurts Slayah.

The scoundrel stares daggers at Heart. "I didn't volunteer for a suicide mission."

Heart rubs the back of her head. "Our odds are way better with you and Karma on the team. Besides, nowhere on the server will be safe if Perfect clears the boss first."

"How can you be sure?" asks Mischief.

"Perfect dreams of clearing the dungeon first. He aims to rally the whole server behind him as their savior."

Mischief sniffs. "A cult leader. Just what every prison needs."

There is more to Perfect than lust for control," Slayah warns. "He intends to finish the game and return to the real world at any cost."

"It's the 'at any cost' part that disturbs me," I add.

Mischief rubs her temples. "I already regret this, but OK. I'm in."

I slide my window shut. "Welcome to the jungle, ladies. Try to keep up."

"Sounds like you fancy yourself the leader, stud. I'll allow it for now. What's the plan?"

"We get out of town before the other prisoners go from spitting at me to stoning me. But first, Heart, can you sell my loot for me? Slayah's, too. He knows a shop that pays top dollar."

"I'd be happy to."

Slayah and I open trade windows and dump our loot into her inventory.

"I'll come along and make sure you don't get fleeced." Mischief points at Slayah and me. "You two get out of town and wait for us along the road. You should be able to track us on the minimap."

Karma raises her hand. "What about me?"

"You're with me. I can't let you out of my sight for five minutes without you spending our savings on crêpes."

"Crêpes are a great idea, Missy. Let's buy five. No, ten."

Mischief facepalms.

"Speaking of food." Slayah passes a few coins to Mischief. "We require traveling rations and water. I suggest enough supplies to cover the five of us for one week. Buy blankets for the two of you. The forests get cold."

Mischief blanches. "We're gonna sleep outside? Ugh. You know ancient man invented houses so gorgeous women like me wouldn't have to rough it, right?"

"The Copper Hoods are after us," I remind her.

"Same here, stud. Me and the dairy cow have been dodging them just fine."

"Think you can dodge them *and* the Golden Dawn?"

She grimaces at my words. "I joined this outfit for protection. I'm sticking around just to see you eat your words for once."

I jerk my thumb over my shoulder. "We'll be outside of town on the east side of the road to the dungeon. Come join us when you've loaded up on supplies. We've got some leveling up to do."

CHAPTER 19

NEW CHOICES

Mischief stabs a robot in the throat with a dagger. Acid hisses at the incision site. Karma's rotating barrels of death gun down three more foes. When there's nothing left of the latest swarm but broken glass on the damp concrete, I turn to Slayah.

"With five of us, grinding monsters is almost too easy."

"Enemy AI seems especially weak in this dungeon. Our foes will increase in complexity and variation as we advance up God's Staircase, requiring greater intraparty coordination to defeat. And our teamwork must be absolutely perfect to survive the boss fight."

"Ugh, we've been at this for hours." Mischief blows out a breath and slumps onto her haunches. "What are we even doing in this stinky sewer?"

Slayah opens his window and manifests a parchment. "We are completing the map."

I gape at him. "You've got Perfect's map?"

"He required me to transcribe the results for him each night. This is a copy, not the original."

"Yeah," I chuckle. "We're not that lucky."

"Where are we headed?" asks Heart. "I'd swear we turned left at the first major intersection and haven't been back to the main tunnel since."

"You are correct. Perfect insisted that the boss room must be located in the farthest depths of the dungeon. I, however, suspect we will find the boss room along the front wall."

Karma looks up from collecting loot bags and gazes at Slayah in wonder. "The front? No way. It's gotta be as far back as possible. That's where you put the best treasures."

"Treasures, perhaps. But recall that defeating the boss opens the next floor. The boss's death must also trigger some means of ascension. It makes sense to place it as close to the front of the sewer as possible so explorers must traverse the entire next level to reach the second dungeon. The outside areas are meant to prepare us for the internal dungeons, after all."

"You're betting it's something like a staircase that'll run from the boss room to the edge of the next step," I infer.

"Precisely. Placing the boss room at the far end of this dungeon could mean we'd exit right in front of the next dungeon's doors. That would be weak game design."

Mischief arches an eyebrow at Slayah. "What if the way up is an elevator on the cliff face? The boss room could be anywhere."

"In that event, the boss placement could be truly random, and there is no point even trying to guess the direction. We would be forced to wander in the dark. That, too, would be poor game design for the starting dungeon. Predictability is key for new players, especially those with no prior gaming experience."

Mischief smirks. "Let me guess. On the outside you were a game dev who got caught with his hand in the cookie jar."

"Creating video games was my goal in life. Incarceration has delayed that ambition, for now."

I point my mace down the dripping tunnel toward the front wall. "So the boss is that way?"

"Perhaps. It's equally possible the boss is on the other side of the entrance, along the right side of the dungeon instead of the left side we are exploring now. That cannot be predicted and must be learned through trial and error."

"So it's fifty-fifty," says Heart. "Either way, Perfect is in the wrong area." She pauses, then adds: "Probably."

Slayah shrugs. "Probably. I suspect we are heading in the correct direction because most players are right-handed and will automatically turn right at the first major intersection. After exploring the right, they'll have to turn around and explore the entire left side. Placing the boss room on the left side would double the first dungeon's playtime."

"If we are getting close to the boss, we'd better check today's progress." I slide open my menu to glance over my stats. *Looking good.* A new tab marked Flair catches my eye. Opening it unfurls multiple options.

Side Step (Acrobatics)—When taking an attack, you may expend stamina to dodge. This movement shifts you from your current position ninety degrees to the target's side.

Bull Strength (Athletics)—Stamina bar depletes at half speed during physical activity.

Fists of Fury (Brawling)—Your unarmed attacks can add one damage attribute (Piercing, Crushing, or Slashing).

Join the Club (Maces)—A sweeping strike that deals damage in an arc and knocks enemies back ten feet.

Merchant's Eye (Perception)—Appraise items and potentially increase their market value.

Not Today (Shields)—Take an attack meant for any party member within 10 feet. All damage is halved and transferred to you.

"Heart, did you get new Flairs?"

"Sure did." Her window shimmers in the dank air. "I have to choose which one to equip."

I peruse my list. "I can only take one of these?"

"No." Slayah opens his menu. "These are all unlocked because of your skill level. You may swap them out, but you can only have one active at a time."

"So I can set a combat Flair for use in the dungeon, then head back to town and equip a merchant Flair when selling items. But I can't use both at the same time."

"Correct. A second slot opens at level eighty."

A section marked Combo Flair beckons at the bottom of the list. Meteor Rush and Siege Breaker are both selected, and it shows I've got five available slots. "Doesn't look like Combo Flair has the level cap."

Mischief jerks her head in my direction. "Combo Flair?"

"Heart, Slayah, and I unlocked a group combo," I explain. "Later, Heart and I unlocked one just for us. Looks like it's tied to the Affinity scores between players."

Mischief slides her window open and scans it with sharp eyes. "I've got level one Affinity with Karma, but that's it. We haven't seen any combo options."

"They pop up when party members unlock the necessary skill ranks. My guess is Cryoblend's market analysts unlock combos when our viewer counts are hot."

Slayah strokes his chin. "Viewers dislike deus ex machina mechanics. But because we must meet the prerequisites first, unlocking a Combo Flair rewards efforts we've already expended."

"It's like tossing a knife into a fistfight," says Mischief.

"Indeed," says Slayah. "They hand us a weapon but let us decide how to use it. Otherwise the combos would become cheap gimmicks weighted toward fan favorites."

"There's another angle you're all missing." Heart's sad tone draws all eyes to her. "This is a prison. Combos unlock based on Affinity and friendship, and we can only use them by trusting each other."

"Rehabilitation." Mischief scoffs. "At my sentencing, the judge told me this game was designed to reform players. The Combo Flair system incentivizes us to learn the magic of friendship. That kind of shit."

"Sounds like their typical crap." I set Not Today as my active Flair and shut my menu. "Don't worry, you and Karma will—"

"Die with the rest of you losers!" ChocolateReaper rushes at us from the darkness. The copper hood pulled over his face doesn't hide the glowing green name over his head.

I raise my shield. "Come at me, you bastard!"

Reaper darts past me. I turn to follow him, but he runs straight through our formation and out the back without drawing a weapon.

The walls echo with thudding footsteps. Forty robots charge from the darkness. They jerk to a halt, and their red eyes fix on me and my party.

"Don't attack them!" My frantic order stays my companions' hands, but the robots throw themselves at us. I absorb the first three strikes on my shield. "We didn't draw their aggro."

"Stealth Flair." Mischief dodges a flurry of steel fists. "Dumps aggro on the nearest player."

I throw my enemies back with a sweep of my shield, but there are too many of them. Their return attacks knock my health down to half.

Heart cries out from somewhere in the melee. Her health bar plummets to the last quarter.

"Fall back to the wall!" Slayah's voice cuts through the din. "Standard formation!" He beats robots with both ends of his bow. Karma's rotary blunderbuss thunders into the enemy ranks, clearing a path for Mischief, who springs to my side.

Heart's fighting her way toward us when a robot strikes at the back of her head. I swing my shield in her direction. The motion doesn't cover the strike, but it does activate Not Today. The robot's fist slams Heart down at my feet, but her health bar remains unchanged. The damage meant for her vanishes from my health bar. *Only one quarter left.*

Mischief grabs my arm. "Come on!"

I'm grateful for my shield straps as I seize Heart by the arm and drag her up. Mischief pulls us both away from the mob. The churning mass of robots surge forward in pursuit.

We make it to the wall. Heart huddles at my back with her blade poised.

Mischief bites a stopper from a bottle. She thrusts the opening to my lips. "Drink!"

I trust her. As the burning taste of cranberries and vinegar plunges down my throat, I block one attack with my shield and parry another with my mace. My throat squeezes shut on the bitter concoction and I cough, but Mischief wraps around me from behind and mashes the bottle against my lips. I've got no choice but to gulp it down as I block another attack.

Beautiful red pixels flood my health bar to nearly full.

Mischief unwinds from me and tends to Heart. "You're good, stud. Now clear me some space."

"With pleasure." I swing my shield and mace in wide arcs. The blows glass robots Karma and Slayah have been chipping away at. Two more bots flank me.

Heart's health bar rises to three-quarters. Her sharp thin blade appears at my left side, jabbing the robots that are double-teaming me in the gut.

Slayah looses a cluster of arrows that glass both robots. "Mischief, clear additional space with your bombs."

The roar of Karma's blunderbuss pales before the explosion that rips through the robots' ranks. Red shards bounce off the walls and ceiling, and even the robots that survive are thrown away from the impact crater.

"Chains," Slayah shouts, "Heart, Meteor Rush the thickest group to your right."

My shield glows. I drop to one knee as Heart charges me. When she leaps on my shield, I hurl her like a comet at the cluster of enemies twenty feet ahead of us. They burst apart in a shower of red glass.

Heart skids to a halt and grins back at me. "I love doing that!"

Slayah nocks three arrows. "Mischief, Karma, hit the robots hard before they can close again." He fires. Each projectile scores a head shot that glasses an enemy.

Karma blasts five more bots apart. Mischief's smaller bombs knock the last few groups around until swirling stars appear above their heads.

"Our foes are now Stunned," Slayah says. "Press the attack."

I bash the nearest robot to glass. "I gotta admit, Slayah. You sound ten times more badass when you're yelling out orders. Where's that confidence the rest of the time?"

Slayah bullseyes the last robot. It erupts into red shards. "Should I be shouting orders at you all the time?"

"Only if you want a kick in the balls." Mischief downs a potion and refills her health. "How the hell did we survive that?"

"Teamwork." I smile at my party. "We pulled together and trusted each other."

Mischief pretends to gag. "I think I'm gonna be sick."

"Don't be that way, Missy." Karma sweeps the smaller woman up in a crushing bear hug. "We can all be besties. Together forever!"

Buried somewhere in Karma's cleavage, Mischief shrieks a muffled stream of profanity.

Ignoring her squirming friend, Karma stares at me. "That Meteor Rush, though. I wanna do that."

"You'll unlock your own combos." I give her a thumbs-up. "Let's keep working together. It'll happen before you know it."

Karma beams.

Mischief finally breaks free. She gives her sheepish friend a tongue lashing as Slayah and Heart gather up their loot bags.

I wander off a bit from the crew. They're laughing and scolding and smiling. Even Slayah is grinning. I'm thinking about what I just said. *Keep working together.*

A knife twists in my heart.

"Dad," I whisper, "I tried to avoid it, but I made some friends. Look at them. They expect me to guide them. I'm going to get these people killed."

I turn away and cover my eyes. "I don't know what to do. Help me, Dad."

The darkness doesn't answer.

CHAPTER 20

SOCIAL DISTANCING

We head back to Geartown in the evening.

"I'll say it again." I stare up at the imposing arch as we cross into the bustling town. "I don't think we should set foot here until early morning."

Mischief huffs. "I don't do early mornings, stud. I intend to conduct business like everyone else. If they don't like it, they can kiss my boot."

"Don't come crying to me if someone pulls a knife on you," I warn.

Her eyes glint like steel. "Let them try. This isn't my first hellhole."

I open a trade window with Heart and dump in all my loot. She accepts with a sad smile. "I'll do my best to get you top dollar, Chains."

"Get whatever you can. It'll be more than I'd get for it."

"Are you going to hide somewhere?" Heart asks.

"Yeah, the alley over there. Come find me when you're all done."

Everyone heads off in a big group, leaving me alone. I shuffle into the dark alley beside the public square and settle in to wait.

It's not long before a smooth voice grates my eardrums. "I tell you, people of Geartown, that I have had enough!"

"What the—? Perfect?" I peer from the alley's mouth. A large crowd has gathered around a wagon parked against the far side of the square. I can just make out Perfect in his fancy black coat and top hat. He strides back and forth on the improvised stage, stomping and gesticulating. The mob at his feet stares up at him in rapt fascination.

He's really fired up. "Enough living in fear! The Copper Hoods prey on us like mad dogs, but I am here to protect you all. I give my solemn word that I will clear this game and get you all home."

Scattered applause rises from the crowd.

"I'll prove it by finishing this first-floor dungeon within the week."

This time, the crowd cheers. Perfect puffs out his chest like a rooster.

When the cheers die down, someone in the front row yells, "Wasn't BrokenChains one of your boys?"

The crowd mutters.

Perfect spits on the stage. "That vagrant joined us for a short time, against my better judgment."

I damn near leap from the alley and go after him. But he's surrounded by hundreds of adoring fans hanging on his every word.

"I tolerated Chains until he turned on us," Perfect continues. "We caught him double-dealing with the Copper Hoods. He killed one of my weakest supporters during his getaway. But don't worry. We will clear this dungeon. We will get you home."

I bite my tongue to keep from shouting. As the mob applauds, I turn on my heel and head to the other end of the alley to wait.

A few minutes later, my party returns. Mischief stomps up to me. "You owe me a fortune, you bastard. Pay up."

My brow furrows. "What's eating you?"

Heart's shoulders droop. "People saw us together in the dungeon. Word has spread, and now Mischief and Karma can't sell their items."

"My crêpes." Karma sniffles. "They're calling to me, but I can't afford them."

Mischief gets up in my face. "Throwing in with a loser like you was the worst mistake in my already reckless life. You owe me restitution!"

I hold her angry gaze for a minute, then look away. "You guys should just leave."

Mischief blinks. "Seriously?"

"I'm dragging you all down. Tell them I conned you, but you wised up to my game and cut me loose. Do whatever you gotta do to get back to normal."

"No way." Heart grabs my elbow. "We've been through too much together. Besides, everyone hates me as much as they hate you."

"And I will not live a life based on deception." Slayah clasps my shoulder. After a couple of seconds, he even makes eye contact. "You could have won favor with Perfect's group by mocking me like the others did. Instead, you became my friend. You did not abandon me for your own profit. I will not abandon you now."

Mischief sighs. "I've got nowhere else to go. Even if I did turn on you, people are scum. They'll make my life hell just because they can. You're the only people who've treated me like a human since I got locked in here."

"And I've had sooo much fun," Karma gushes.

"Last chance for you guys to back out. I get people killed. My own father is ashamed of me. You sure you want to do this?"

"Let's show 'em we're the best." Karma stretches her hand into the middle of the group.

"You know I'm with you." Heart smiles at me and lays her hand on Karma's.

Slayah sticks in his hand next.

Mischief shrugs and adds her hand. "Guess I've got no choice."

I sigh. "OK." I add my hand to the top of the pile. "We're all besties, I guess."

"Yuck." Mischief curls her lip. "Don't get all mushy on us, stud."

Heart and Karma giggle.

"I suggest we leave town." Slayah glances up and down the alley. "The crowd is dispersing, and we might become targets."

"We'll hit the dungeon at four a.m. tomorrow."

Mischief looks like she just bit a lemon.

"We need to beat Perfect and his crew inside," I explain. "Unless you want to fight them at the door."

"Not especially," Mischief grumbles.

"It's settled." I turn to exit the alley. "Let's head for the woods and set up camp."

CHAPTER 21

RESCUE AND A JOB

Two huge spiders with cyborg legs duck under Karma's booming blunderbuss. Their hydraulic pincers latch onto her arms.

Karma struggles, but the spiders hold on. "*Help!* They've got me!"

"I'm coming, Karma!" Heart's rapier flashes with surgical precision. Both cyborg spiders explode and coat the mossy concrete with glitter.

"Whew, thanks." Karma hefts her enormous gun and racks up some revenge kills on a skeleton cluster pouring in from a side passage.

"Mischief," Slayah warns, "you have exposed yourself."

"You'd like that, wouldn't you?" Mischief slashes a giant spider to death with her dagger, but another one bites her butt. "Ouch! Damn thing poisoned me."

Slayah glasses the offending spider with an arrow to its eight-eyed head. "I told you to watch out."

Mischief points a dagger at him. "Who are you to tell me how to fight?"

I smash a robot in its brass face and shoot Mischief a backward glance. "Just our strategist. He saved our bacon when ChocolateReaper hit us with a monster parade, remember?"

"Sure, but that doesn't mean he gets to order us around." The scoundrel tosses two small vials over her shoulder. A chain of explosions blasts down the tunnel, glassing the last four monsters.

"I give advice," Slayah corrects her, "not orders. Ignoring it may come back to bite you."

Mischief rubs her butt. "Point taken." She downs an antidote to cure her poisoned status.

Heart blinks at the archer. "Was- was that a joke?"

"A turn of phrase," Slayah says flatly.

"Nerding out on war games made Slayah a tactical genius." Mischief turns to me. "Where'd you learn to fight?"

"The PRC Central Valley," I say like a tourism board commercial. "Dust and meth as far as the eye can see. I helped a family friend run her little liquor store. The cops are too busy policing social media to handle real crime. You wanna survive as a business, gotta get used to fighting off thieves yourself."

"I know what that's like." Karma hops and waves her hand excitedly. "I ran my dad's car repair shop near Fresno. Tons of bozo customers tried to skip out on their bills. I had to crack skulls so my brothers and sisters could get enough to eat."

Heart smiles. "You've got siblings?"

"Nine brothers and sisters. I'm the oldest. Been keeping everyone in line since Mom passed and Dad got hurt."

"I'm sorry." Heart winces. "Didn't mean to hit a sore spot."

Karma winks. "It's OK. I had all those brothers and sisters to take care of. Never a dull moment in Karma's world."

Slayah glances up and down the tunnel, then points to our left. "It's late in the evening. We could head outside to sleep in the forest, but I have seen no other parties following the front wall."

"We do seem to be off the beaten path," I agree. "Could we sleep in here? Someplace with no monster spawns, that is."

Slayah checks his parchment map and points to our left. "We will find a room sixty yards in that direction. It even has a door we can barricade from the inside."

A boom rolls down the tunnel. When it passes, the clamor of wild battle fills my ears. Voices filter through the din.

"I'm out of antidotes!"

"Backs together! We can still survive this!"

Slayah trains his dark eyes down the tunnel. "It appears someone is in trouble."

"Do we check it out?" Heart turns to me. "It could be the Copper Hoods laying a trap for us. They know we rescue people."

"Could be. But no way am I letting paranoia turn me into a callous slimeball like Perfect."

Mischief looks up from inspecting her loot. "Hey, stud. I didn't sign on to help randos."

"Be grateful I decided to help the last two randos I came across."

Mischief clamps her mouth shut.

I lead the party down the tunnel at a jog. "Keep your eyes open."

The battle sounds swell to deafening volume as we turn a corner and spot three warriors covered head to toe in bright red armor. I recognize them from town: TRexFromSpace, TacoKing, and Chainsawlogy. They stand back to back against a horde of chittering spiders.

"Karma, get their attention."

"You got it, Chains." Karma's blunderbuss rakes the spiders' back ranks. Half the mob turns and leaps at our heads.

"Behind me!" I raise my shield, and my party ducks into its shadow. A dozen bladed legs send shocks up my arm. Heart and Mischief stab the beasts that try to scuttle around us. Karma and Slayah open fire at point-blank range. Broken glass litters the concrete.

"Cut a path toward us," I shout to the three red warriors. They bull rush in V formation through the stabbing, biting horde.

"Mischief, get some potions ready for them."

"Fine, stud, but you're reimbursing my losses."

The three warriors spill into our formation. Mischief shoves a healing potion at each of them. They quaff the crimson liquid like frat boys at a kegger.

TacoKing punches my shoulder. "Nice timing. Let's crush some bugs. TRex, Chainsaw, form up around Chains. Meatshield formation!"

147

"Maximum carnage, baby!" TRex bellows through his visor slits.

Chainsaw strikes his red chest. "*For the glory of the empire!*"

As weird as the two of them sound, TRex and Chainsaw's two-handed sword skills are no joke. They carve into the spider lines with reckless abandon.

Golden light fills the tunnel behind me. TacoKing leaps over our frontline and slams his enormous battle-ax into the tunnel floor. Cracks spread from the impact as the earth shakes. Spiders across the tunnel flip onto their backs and wriggle their legs.

"Karma, Mischief," I yell, "spread some damage!"

The girls unleash their full AoE effects. Blunderbuss shots and poppers reduce the spider ranks by half before they flip back over and charge again.

We press forward to meet TacoKing, who's chopping at spiders like a lumberjack clear-cutting trees. His two buddies churn through spiders at top speed to rejoin their ally. Together, the eight of us smash the remaining enemies into a sea of red glass.

TacoKing stows his ax on his back and extends his hand. "Thanks for the assist, king. You crushed those beasties." He clasps my hand in a viselike grip.

I respond in kind. "Gotta help those in need. Why'd you guys bite off more than you can chew?"

"Those assholes in copper headgear led the parade right to us," says Taco.

"You hit the spiders?" I ask.

"Nah, the thugs kicked aggro onto us. Dunno how, but screw that noise, man."

"Look, you know I'm *the* BrokenChains, right? Most people would be spitting on me right now."

Taco taps his slitted helmet. "Ain't my habit to hate someone just 'cause I'm told to. And that Perfect guy's a douche. I don't take his word for nothin'."

"Glad to hear it. We're close to clearing the dungeon. Wanna team up with us?"

"Negatory. I won't judge you based on hearsay, but I won't volunteer to draw the hate brigade, if you feel me."

I nod. "Yeah, I feel you."

"That's not to say we're ungrateful. If you ever need help, just whistle. We'll come runnin'."

"Thanks, Taco."

"No sweat, man. All right TRex, Chainsaw. Back to the grind."

TRex pulls a slick dance spin. "I love the smell of entrails in the morning."

Chainsaw pounds his gauntleted fist to his metal breast. "*May the emperor shine upon our campaign!*"

Taco leans in close and whispers, "Chainsaw's a role-player. Just go with it." He shouts to his crew. "All right, boys, roll out!"

The three warriors stride off down the dark tunnel.

Mischief snorts. "We meet all the best psychos."

The five of us hoof it to Slayah's designated safe room. He shuts the door behind us, sealing our party into a garage-size concrete chamber with grimy walls.

I dismiss my weapons into my inventory and take a seat in the middle of the cold floor. "I'm beat. We cleared a huge chunk of the western dungeon today."

Slayah consults his map again. "Indeed. I suspect we draw nearer our goal. The new spider enemies indicate a change, at least."

Heart shivers. "Miserable vermin."

I laugh. "You don't like bones, and you don't like spiders. Anything else?"

"Yes." She smiles at me. "Smart guys who point out my weaknesses."

Karma kneels in the middle of the room, dumps some logs out of her inventory, then lights them with a torch. "Can't have a hot dinner without heat."

"Hot dinner?" Slayah perks up.

"Yup, just a sec." Karma manifests a big pot next. She nestles it into the burning logs and adds a bottle of cream, a bag of shrimp, and some potatoes. By the time she sprinkles in a handful of herbs, I'm salivating.

"While you're all playing house, I'll keep watch." Mischief starts to open the door, but Slayah presses it shut again. "What's your damage?" she snaps.

"You intend to wait alone in the tunnel?"

"Yeah, so?"

"Two large gangs are hunting us. In addition, every inmate in this prison identifies you with a suspected killer. Sound will not carry well through that thick door. If a malicious party happens by, are you prepared to die without us hearing your screams?"

Mischief grimaces. "You guys would see my health bar drop, right?"

"Perhaps, if we gave your status our undivided attention. But that would rather defeat the point of you striking off alone."

"I . . ." Mischief stammers. "I . . ."

"That is what I thought." Slayah manifests four anvils from his inventory. They clunk against the door.

My jaw drops. "Where did you—?"

"I purchased them yesterday for just such an occasion."

Mischief tugs on the door. It hardly rattles. "Fine, I guess that'll do." She slinks back to the fire and flops down beside Karma.

"Cheer up, Missy. The shrimp chowder is ready. Give me your bowl."

Mischief's knees muffle her sulky voice. "Ain't got a bowl."

"Even my littlest brother remembers his bowl, Missy. But you can borrow one of mine. It's got flowers." Karma pulls out the brightest fuchsia bowl I've ever seen. Sure enough, it's covered in painted flowers. She ladles a huge portion of savory-smelling chowder into the bowl and shoves it into Mischief's hands. "Some hot food will turn that frown upside down."

"How can you say that without wanting to kick your own ass?" Mischief sniffs the bowl with a suspicious look.

Karma dishes up for the rest of us. I take an experimental sip. Smooth warmth tickles my tongue. I gulp a hearty mouthful. And a second. I don't pause for breath until my bowl is half-empty. "Karma, this soup is killer."

Slayah hasn't even paused for breath. His eyes are bulging, so I yank his bowl away. He claws to get it back even as he gasps for air.

Heart takes a long sip and hums in appreciation. "Makes me feel all warm inside. Karma, you're a better cook than I am. This is wonderful."

Karma practically glows. "Thanks, everyone. I started leveling up my Cooking skill right away. Taking the Chef profession was a no-brainer."

"Profession?" I try to talk and drink at the same time. "What do you mean, profession?"

"I hit rank four hundred on Cooking and unlocked a whole set of options and menus. The description called it a 'secondary job.'"

"Meaning there may be primary jobs." Slayah strokes his chin. "Curious. I wonder when combat jobs might unlock. But it would be smart to level up noncombat skills and unlock our own professions. That may provide desperately needed income, given our pariah status."

"Let's see. What job would I do?" I flip open my menu and peruse my skills. "One of my highest is Perception. And I already unlocked Merchant's Eye. I've got experience running a liquor store. Maybe I can get Merchant to unlock. If you guys don't mind, hand over all your gear that can be appraised."

They each trade over a handful of items gathered from the last battle. I appraise them all. I gain ranks fast to start, but the increases slow and finally stop.

Merchant skill increased to 400.
Merchant profession now available.

"Hey, I unlocked Merchant as a secondary job." I open the menus and read over the information. "Wow, I can buy my own shop."

"Usually you start small." Mischief holds her thumb and forefinger close together. "Like those carts inside the front gate. The Merchant profession is how players build their businesses."

The mention of going into business plants an idea in my head. "Perfect told me the Copper Hoods' camgirl channels earn them real-world money."

"That is sadly correct," says Slayah. "Viewers can pay inmates real currency through the Open Market."

I squint at my window. "I'm not seeing that option under the Merchant profession."

"The Open Market can only be accessed from hubs in town or at designated guild houses. Shop ownership is a prerequisite for selling on the Market."

"Don't tell me you two sleazeballs are starting an online brothel," Mischief sasses.

"No." I turn back to Slayah. "Players can sell other stuff for cash, right?"

"Certainly. Game goods can be exchanged for real money and vice versa. The sale of rare drops and custom-crafted items constitutes a lucrative market."

I cup my chin in thought.

"Crafting may yield valuable products," says Slayah. "Can I tinker with your shield?"

"Sure." I drag and drop my Steel Kite Shield Rank 4 icon into the trade window he opens, then hit **Accept**. It manifests in his lap. He pulls out a set of engineer's tools and goes to work on it.

"Speaking of tinkering . . ." Mischief busts out an alchemy set with a rack of glass vials and a bubbling mixture in a twisting tube. "I'm working on expanding my repertoire. Bombs and healing potions are great, but I want to find ways to enhance our abilities." She pulls a dark yellow potion from the rack. "Slayah, you're working on Weaponsmithing right? Drink this."

Slayah takes the vial and bolts down the drink. He tosses the empty glass back to Mischief and picks up his tools. Within moments, he's built a compartment in the center of my shield with whirring gears protruding from the gap. "Incredible. My speed has doubled. Thank you."

Mischief looks smug. "Just a taste of my growing power. After Karma unlocked her Chef profession, I chose Alchemist. My potions will revolutionize the way people survive this game. If they're willing to pay my steep prices."

"Got one of those for me?" I ask.

"Alchemical ingredients don't grow on trees, stud." Mischief packs up her chemistry set. "Some of them have such low drop rates, I'd have to spend the rest of my sentence farming to make enough potions for the boss fight."

"My crafting efforts will encounter the same roadblock," Slayah says as he fiddles with my shield.

Heart pulls a bolt of cloth from her inventory along with a needle and thread. "I've been leveling up my Tailoring skill. It hasn't unlocked a profession yet, but it'll cover our basic clothing needs."

Mischief elbows her. "And you can make lacy undies to sell in Chains's shop."

Heart blushes.

I get us back on topic. "What made you choose Tailoring?"

Heart draws up her knees. After a few seconds, she sighs. "I did a lot of sewing for my daughter at home. We didn't have much money, so I made all her stuffed animals."

"Where's your daughter now?" asks Karma.

"With my sister. At least, she was before I got sentenced. My husband died, so she's lost both parents now."

The room falls silent. Karma cleans up the pot and soup in a flash by absorbing it into her inventory. We gather around the warm fire.

"Amazing how even in digital, flames are soothing." I stare into the burning logs and let my shoulders relax.

$$\bullet \ \bullet \ \bullet \ \bullet$$

"Chains." Slayah's voice wakes me from my food coma. He releases his tools and hands me the shield. "It is finished. Give this a try."

I accept the trade and scan the item's stats.

Clockwork Steel Kite Shield
Armor rating 270
Traps enemy weapons for 3 seconds on successful parry.

"Trapping enemy weapons might not be too useful in dungeon battles, but it'll give me a serious edge against Perfect's goons. Thanks, Slayah."

"I can provide better upgrades as we progress," Slayah promises. "And I hope to craft entirely new weapons for the party."

"Good," I murmur. "We'll be fighting for our lives from here on out."

Slayah nods. "The difficulty curve will rise steeply as we near the boss room. To have any hope of clearing the dungeon, we must find a way to acquire supplies."

I pull out my blanket and lie down beside the fire. "We'll head into town first thing in the morning. I've got an idea for how to make us some money."

CHAPTER 22

A LITTLE PLACE OF MY OWN

We get most of the way to town before the sun pokes above the mountains. Mischief stumbles along, groggily munching a still-piping fried egg sandwich courtesy of Karma.

We reach Geartown's front gate and run right into Perfect and his growing crew. My party of five now faces twenty armored Knights with twitchy weapon hands. Rainpig and LaserToast finger their blades and shoot me jackal grins.

My party starts to draw, but I hold up my hand. "Let them make the first move."

Perfect strides to the head of his mob. "Chains," he grandstands. "Fancy meeting you here. Come back to murder someone else?"

"Hello, Perfect. Going out to meet your stooge Reaper?"

"Spouting baseless slander just makes you look worse, Chains." Perfect grips his sabers. "Putting you down would be a mercy to you and your intended victim."

I nod at the NPC soldiers twenty feet away. "There's plenty of places to kill each other, but not in front of the gate guards. First one to attack draws aggro from two level-nine-hundred-ninety-nine NPCs."

Perfect glances over his shoulder. "They're here to prevent monsters from entering the city. Ironic that they'd keep me from doing the same."

I prod my face. "Come on over here and plant a slap on my cheek. I dare you."

Perfect releases his saber hilts. "You think I've got time to waste on you?"

"Your copper-top thugs sure do."

"Nice try, Chains. Everyone knows you work with the Copper Hoods."

"Say what you need to in front of your squad, Perfect. We both know the truth."

Heart steps to my side. "And so do I."

Perfect smirks. "I'd almost forgotten about you. If not for the blessed quiet in the absence of your yapping, I'd never know you left." He glances over my shoulder. "And Slayah. Found someone else to annoy? Be careful. A brute like Chains may express his annoyance with more than words."

Slayah looks Perfect dead in the eye. The frock-coated slime flinches.

"Your ego-driven crusade won't accomplish anything, Chains," Perfect blusters. "All you'll do is lead your little band to ruin like the killer you are."

I stifle a flinch of my own. "You say I'm a killer? That's right. But you're worse. You sicced your crew on us to hide your secret."

"I don't have time for this." Perfect turns back to his guild. "Leave the dogs to bark for now. We'll deal with them after I clear the boss and secure our server's future."

The Knights march around us, sneering. Rainpig and LaserToast make feints for their weapons. Mischief reaches for a dagger, but Karma holds her back. Pigman and Toast chortle.

When the Golden Dawn passes, Heart lets out a huge breath. "Scumbags. We gotta clear that boss first, or Perfect really will have us murdered."

"Let's go." I lead the party through the front gate into Geartown.

"Where are we headed?" asks Heart.

"I'm gonna open a shop," I explain. "How do I do that?"

"Find an open one and buy in," says Mischief. "I'll show you." She turns right and leads me to a line of carts against the wall. Most have eye-catching umbrellas, but a few unclaimed ones languish at the end. "Take your pick, stud."

I walk over to the first available cart and poke a glowing purple dot on the countertop. A menu pops open.

Welcome to the Merchant's Network!
Purchase this shop: 10,000 gold.

"Oof, that buy-in cost, though. Can't I just pay with one of my kidneys?"

Karma sighs. "Yeah, that's why I haven't opened a bakery yet. Mischief won't let me spend so much in one place."

"No, I won't let you start a bakery because you'd eat all your merchandise."

"Hehe." Karma rubs her coverall-clad tummy. "I totally would."

I bite the bullet and spend the fortune. Almost every penny I've made from countless battles vanishes in a blink, but the shop lights up with fireworks.

Congratulations, you are now a shop owner!
We see this is your first shop. Do you want to take the tutorial?

"No time. Just wanna sell and go." I click off the pop-up, and it disappears. "OK, everybody hand me all your loot."

A swell of gratitude heats my face when my friends instantly oblige. I drag our items into the storefront. "I think I'll undersell the competition by ten percent."

Mischief laughs. "You're hated across the whole server. I'd say undercut by twenty. That's big enough to pull in the schmucks with weak morals. Not every inmate has a heart of gold like me."

"Twenty leaves our margins slim."

"But gets people used to buying from you. Then you slide your prices up by five points next time."

"They throw you in here for dealing drugs, Mischief?"

The scoundrel grins slyly. "I'll take that as a compliment."

Loading our whole cache takes a few minutes. When I'm done, we've got nearly a hundred unique listings floating on the open market.

"OK, that's all of them." I close the shop menu and step back. A flimsy red umbrella sprouts from the wooden cart's top, and an **OPEN** sign pops onto the counter. "My shop looks hideous. Guess we're aiming for the shut-in demographic. Mischief, can you show me a Market hub?"

"Sure, stud." She guides me down the road to a wide alcove holding a crystal ball on a pedestal. "Just touch your hand to the glass."

I stretch out my hand. The moment my fingertips brush the glass, a huge window opens up and sprawls across my vision. "Slayah, can inmates link their shops to the bank accounts of people on the outside?"

"Of course. The PRC is not about to pass up a ready source of tax revenue."

I flip through a few menus and find what I'm looking for. Slayah's right. I can deposit my share of the shop's proceeds to an outside account.

Wish I could send a message, Mom. Hope this money lets you know I haven't abandoned you and Sis. I enter my mother's financial information and click **Accept**.

I step away from the hub, and the window closes. "That's it. All our loot's listed, and we'll split the profits evenly."

"The system automatically links our names to your shop on stream," Slayah points out. "The more viewers we attract, the higher your name will go in the server's popularity ranking, and the higher sales volume we can expect. Even inmates who despise you will likely want to buy from the popular merchant. That is how major corporate brands work, after all."

"And I'll get my crêpes!" Karma pumps her fist. Her bulging biceps comically clash with her expression of girlish glee.

Mischief bonks her on the head. "Dummy. We need every coin we can get to finance this boss fight. All our hard work means nothing if we die in the final room."

"Come on." I turn back toward the gate. "Let's see how many goods sell while we're in the dungeon today."

CHAPTER 23

PRESSURE COOKER

"Whew!" Karma wipes sweat from her forehead. "Another spider squad put to bed. I'm toast."

"Same here." Mischief slides down the stone wall to sit on the mossy floor. "We've been at this all day. I say it's dinner time."

Slayah consults his parchment. "We made excellent progress today. Those new spider enemies we've encountered interest me. I suspect—"

"Wait." My sharp tone cracks through the tunnel. Two lurking shapes withdraw down a side tunnel and disappear.

"Copper Hoods." The name gives even Slayah's voice a hard edge.

Mischief stands up. "Karma and I will scout out our back trail."

"Good idea," I say. "No telling what those thugs might pull."

The two women pad down the tunnel.

I seat myself on the moss carpet across from Heart. Slayah joins us.

"I'm glad we have a chance to talk," Heart tells me.

"Yeah? What's on your mind?"

"You." She blushes. "What I mean is, you've been distracted today."

"Have I?"

Slayah gives me a dry look. "You did not see that last spider until it jumped on your head."

I rub my hair. "Yeah. Guess I am a little out of it."

Heart nods. "Just between old prison friends, what's going on?"

"I'm gonna get you guys killed."

Slayah scans my face. "How so?"

I heave a sigh. "We had zero sales today."

Heart's auburn eyebrows form a V above her nose. "That's it? I didn't take you for a mercenary."

"No, that's not it. I set up my merchant account to give Mom and Sis my share, and I failed them again. One-fifth of zero is zero."

Heart's face softens. "That's not true, Chains."

"It is mathematically true," Slayah cuts in.

I ignore him. "Let's face it. I left my family high and dry when I got locked up, and I can't even help them pick up the pieces."

Heart bites her lip. "You're a good son for trying. I'm sure sales will pick up as we draw more viewers."

"Almost definitely," says Slayah. "Clearing the boss should draw top ratings."

I hold my head. "That's if we clear the boss. My plan to help my family failed. What's to say my plan to beat the boss won't, too?"

"You can't quit now," says Heart. "We only got this far because of you."

"Because of me, you're all outcasts. You can't even earn a living the normal way anymore. That's not gonna get better. A week from now, people will spit at you like they do at me. It would be best for you guys if I pack up and leave."

Slayah shrugs. "The social issue should resolve itself when we clear the first dungeon."

"You don't get it. I failed my dad more times than I can count. I'll fail you, too."

"You believe you failed your father." Slayah shakes his head. "Why is that important?"

"What the hell? Your father is everything, man. Don't you get that?"

"I did not have a father. You, on the other hand, have made yours a millstone. I push forward regardless of what people think or say about me. If you have the strength of your convictions, you must do the same."

"It's not that easy, man."

"I assure you, Chains, that it is. Answer this: Do your mother and sister have the luxury of waiting while you wallow in self-pity?"

I grit my teeth. "No. Of course they don't."

"So instead of using every resource at your disposal to help them, you are considering throwing away your only friends and sulking alone. On a server full of enemies who hate you. Your only hope of getting home to your family is to clear this game as fast as possible. Instead, you indulge in despair. It appears your goal is not to protect your family, but to be perfect in your dead father's eyes."

I punch Slayah in the face. The blow knocks him off his butt and onto his back.

"Chains!" Heart shrieks. "Slayah, are you all right?"

Slayah stares up at me and smiles. "You hit me when I pointed out your hypocrisy because you loathe yourself."

The urge to hit him again clenches my fist.

Heart kneels at Slayah's side. "Stop it, Chains. Can't you see you're proving Perfect right?"

The disappointment in her voice stops me cold, and I just see my friend laid out on the ground. I grab his hand and pull him back up to a sitting position. "Sorry, man."

"No harm done. See?" He points an espresso finger at his floating green health bar. "You are hardly tough enough to damage the great Slayah."

I want to smile, but the truth weighs too heavily on me. Heart rests her hand on my arm.

I gaze at the ground. "It's just frustrating how every time I start to pull ahead, somebody jams a stick in my spokes."

"What do you intend to do about it?" asks Slayah.

"We're baaack!" Karma and Mischief's return spares me the humiliation of admitting I don't have a clue what I'm doing.

Mischief sashays into our midst. "Hate to say it, but Slayah was right. Those spies met up with a squad of Hoods."

"Were you followed?" asks Slayah.

"Yeah." Mischief waves her arms around. "The whole gang's here—invisible! Before you take that literally, no. Me and the dairy cow beat it before they saw us."

A terrifying realization hits me like a truck. "We have to clear this dungeon tomorrow."

Mischief gives a choking laugh. "Excuse me?"

I look to Slayah. "We're getting close to the boss room, right?"

"Yes, the preponderance of spider enemies all but confirms it."

"The Hoods are on to us, which means Perfect will bring his cult this way." I eye my party sternly. "If we don't kill the boss tomorrow, he will."

Karma wilts. "Game over."

Mischief throws up her hands. "But we're not equipped to handle the boss."

Slayah frowns. "That is true. In our current state of unpreparedness, the odds of suffering a party wipe approach one in one."

"What if we pool all our money to buy supplies?" asks Heart.

"Spending the last of our coin at NPC shops may equip us sufficiently to survive the battle," Slayah says, "but it would leave us no margin of error."

"So we gotta pitch a perfect game to win." The decision's gravity pushes me onto my back.

"OK," says Heart, "then that's what we do."

The group goes quiet. Karma breaks the silence first. "We can do it."

"Theoretically, yes," says Slayah. "The opportunity to test my calculations is worth the risk. I vote with Chains."

Mischief cradles her head. "This group is insane!" She laughs. "But that includes me. So yeah, let's do Chains's crazy plan."

I stand back up. "You four head to town before the shops close and buy what you can. We'll meet back at our usual forest camp. Better turn in early because we leave this stair tomorrow, one way or another."

CHAPTER 24

A DUEL IN THE DARK

We're so exhausted when we bed down under the trees that we sleep until 7:00 a.m. No one mentions that our oversleeping gave Perfect a two-hour head start, but we all know it. By the time we reach the dungeon doors, my heart is pounding.

Slayah swipes his menu open and presses an unseen button. A rapier with a pistol grip and twin barrels flanking the blade appears in his hand. "I made this for you, Heart. It's called a burstblade."

Heart takes the gift. The rapier on her hip disappears, and the burstblade's sheath appears in its place. She gives the sword a few practice swings and raises her eyebrows in surprise. "How did you get the balance so perfect, Slayah?"

"I added a few accessories to the hilt, including a weighted pommel. The Weaponsmith profession allows me to create a range of gear for each of us—or it would, given adequate resources."

"You'll have all the resources you need after we clear the boss." I address my party. "Perfect and his goons are probably in the western area right now, closing in on the boss room. We need to beat them to the prize."

"Who's to say Honest Abe hasn't snuffed the boss already?" grouses Mischief.

"The system would almost certainly have notified us had someone opened the second stair," says Slayah.

I take a deep breath. "Perfect wants to be god-emperor of this prison. If he wins, his cult will swell and come for us. We clear the boss before he does, or we die."

Heart looks at each of us in turn. "We're not would-be monarchs like Perfect, and that's our advantage. Each of us has a reason to get home."

"Except me." Slayah looks serious. "I prefer God's Staircase to the real world."

"OK," says Heart, "each of us has a reason to get home, except Slayah, who's in it for the nerd cred."

Everyone shares a laugh, even Slayah. The tension doesn't leave my shoulders though.

Mischief winks at us. "You weirdos haven't got me killed yet. Guess I'll stick around until something better comes along."

"And I'm totes ready for some crêpes when we're done. Chains is gonna buy me twenty in one sitting."

I can't help but laugh. "You got it, Karma. All the crêpes you can eat."

She looks floored. "How . . . how many is that? Gosh, I need to find out."

"Then you'd better survive," Mischief scolds her. "No getting killed. Not any of you."

"Deal. Not one death." This time, I stick my arm out first. The others stack their hands on top of mine. "We'll get through this together."

Heart drops her hand and frowns. "One edge Perfect's guild has on us is a team name. Our guild needs one, too."

"Oh, I know." Karma raises her hand. "The Crêpe Masters!"

Mischief bops her. "Absolutely not, you big goof. Do you ever think with your brain instead of your stomach?"

"Oww. I can't help it if crêpes are the best."

"Retribution." All eyes turn to me. "For Perfect, for Reaper, and for the PRC that put us here. The government wants us to die in their death game. Perfect wants us out of his way, even if he has to murder us. We'll clear this game and make all their lives miserable along the way."

"Retribution." Slayah rolls the word around in his mouth. "I agree."

Heart nods. Mischief and Karma each give me a thumbs-up.

"Retribution it is," I confirm. "Let's head in and dish some out."

We weave deep into the reeking dungeon, following Slayah's map westward. Low-level skeletons and robots easily fall to our advance. We round a bend into an unexplored area.

And come face-to-face with Perfect and his Knights. All twenty of them glare at us as we skid to a halt on red glass filling a wide intersection lined with blue crystal spikes.

"The spiders infesting this area display uncommon strength and cunning." Perfect swaggers into the no-man's land between our two groups. "You'd best leave further exploration to us."

"Fat chance." I get in his face. "This is our hunting ground. Go strut somewhere else, prick."

Perfect's face darkens. He leans in to whisper, "Is that any way to speak to this server's new ruler?"

"Fishing for an apology, Your Majesty?" I scoff.

"I gave you every chance to make amends, Chains. Now it's too late. I've found a replacement."

"You found *another* guy better than you?"

"Ingrate," he snarls. "I found you mired in self-pity and molded you into a semblance of a man. Even after you betrayed me, you had only to admit your guilt and ask for clemency."

"I wouldn't ask you to suck on my ass if a snake bit it."

Perfect clicks his teeth. "That's your fatal sin, Chains—pride. It will be your undoing. Your former paymaster learned that lesson and is ready to atone."

I furl my brow. "My what?"

A wall of muscle clad in black leather walks out of the crowd. Two hefty mace handles jut above his back. A dark ponytail drapes his shoulder.

"ChocolateReaper?" A laugh escapes my throat. "Your top hat's on too tight if you think hiring Reaper proves he doesn't work for you."

Reaper bows his head. "Drop the act, Chains. It's over. I told the Knights everything when I surrendered to them."

The watching crowd spins around me. "What?"

"Everybody knows the Golden Dawn's gonna clear the dungeon first." Reaper sighs. "My crew couldn't compete anymore, so I turned myself in to Perfect."

Rage burns away my confusion. "Liar! You've been working for Perfect all along. I bet he put you up to this."

"Do drop the pretense, Chains," Perfect lectures. "As a condition of his rehabilitation, Reaper confessed all his crimes—including hiring you to spy on me."

Reaper chuckles. "The loser couldn't even do that right."

"I'm forced to agree," says Perfect. "Stop deluding yourself, Chains. You don't have what it takes to save the people of God's Staircase."

"If you mean I'm not a sociopath with a Napoleon complex like you, you're right. I'm no savior, but I'll sure as hell wreck your little Jonestown."

Perfect heaves a weary breath. "Now you're just embarrassing yourself. One last chance: own up to your crimes like a man, and I'll let you and your cronies leave the dungeon. Persist in obstructing this server's liberation, and my guild will mingle your band's glass with the spiders'."

My gaze takes in the grim-faced Knights, my huddled friends, and the number in the corner of my vision.

Viewer Count: 180,000

I raise my saber. "Let me fight Reaper," I yell loud enough for the folks at home to hear.

Perfect blinks. "Pardon?"

"Trial by combat. If I win, you let us go. The two groups split up in opposite directions."

A grin splits Perfect's face. "And if Reaper wins, you die, and your team joins my guild for the final push."

"And after we kill the boss, you kill us!" Heart snaps.

"Perhaps, if you prove as obstinate as your leader." Perfect's eyes bore into mine. "Do you accept?"

"I've been itching to kick Copper-top's ass since day one. Get out of my way."

"Reaper!" Perfect barks. "Earn your redemption. Smear him into pâté."

"Dreams do come true." Reaper smirks, unracks his geared maces, and flexes his whole body.

"Whoa, I wish I could flex like that."

"Quiet, Karma," hisses Mischief. "Be careful, stud. Dude's got biceps on his biceps."

Reaper bears down on me like a freight train. I leap back, and both maces split the ground where I'd been standing. Concrete chips pepper my legs.

"By all means," gloats Reaper, "let's make the fun last."

He swings at me again. I block the first mace, and the impact numbs my shield arm. His second mace bats my saber aside and crunches into my shoulder, draining 20 percent of my health.

I dodge back to get some space. Reaper lunges and swings at me again. I duck under his humming mace, but he kicks me across the intersection.

"Chains," Slayah cries. "Do not touch the wall!"

I land on my feet and skid backward. The crystal spikes reach out to skewer me. I slam the tip of my shield into the ground and grind to a halt inches from the gleaming spears.

My weapon's not working. I swap it out for my second shield. Reaper's maces slam down and rattle my shoulders in their sockets.

Reaper shifts his stance with a grunt and attacks again. His maces spark against my steel shields three times. He thrusts the left mace's spiked tip into my gut and knocks off another 10 percent of my health. His follow-up swing flies over my defenses to ring my head like a bell.

I'm down to 40 percent health, and I haven't even touched him yet. Instead of taking his next attack on my shield, I turn and sprint across the intersection.

Perfect's bubbling laughter follows me. "What's the matter, Chains? Realized you're outclassed?"

"Nowhere to run," taunts Reaper. "Nowhere to hide." His rapid footsteps pound the floor behind me.

I open my menu and switch my active Flair to Side Step. Reaper catches up. I deflect both his strikes and leap to my right. Side Step activates and shifts me to Reaper's left side. Before he can turn, I bash my right shield into his head. His health bar dips by 10 percent.

Reaper's left mace crashes into my clockwork shield. I press the trigger in the handle, and with a grinding noise, the blade grabber latches onto one of the gears embedded in his mace.

Enemy weapon captured for 3 seconds.

I ram my free shield into Reaper's midsection three times. His health drops to 70 percent. He lifts his left arm, pulling me off my feet. Reaper swipes his right mace at my legs. I reflexively bend my knees, and the strike blurs under them.

My shield releases the mace with a metallic shriek. I land hard on the concrete. Reaper kicks me again. This time I have to claw the ground to keep from rolling into the opposite spike wall.

I've got 30 percent health to his 70 percent. And Reaper's wise to my trick. He stalks toward me.

I release the steel shield and draw my mace. While I'm at it, I change my Flair to Join the Club. "Come get some!"

"I'll take the whole thing!"

Reaper charges. I block his swing and step right. He turns and pistons his left mace into my stomach, reducing my health to 10 percent.

I veer right again, and again he turns to follow me. I swing my mace and activate Join the Club. The blue arc only takes him down to 65 percent health, but the shock wave hurls him onto the wall he's turned his back to. Crystal spikes erupt from his chest, and Enchanted's last moments flash before my eyes.

Like the girl he murdered, Reaper stares at the point protruding from his sternum. Unlike her, he survives impalement with 5 percent health.

He staggers off the spikes, and I meet him with my shield. The memory of Enchanted's dying scream urges me to give him one last fatal push.

I can do it. I can end his reign of terror. All it will wake is one little shove. His eyes meet mine and I can see the plea in them. For mercy he's never once dished out.

I pull my shield back and take aim at his chest.

"Chains," Heart says softly from behind me. "You proved Reaper wrong. Don't prove Perfect right."

Reaper sways feebly before me. I clamp my jaw tight. "You move, and I bash you right back onto the spikes. Clear?"

To his credit, Reaper's voice doesn't waver. "Clear."

"I beat your champion, Perfect. Now honor your word."

Rage inflames Perfect's voice. "You're free to go. Which direction do you want?"

"Slayah?" I ask my tactician.

"We choose north from here," Slayah says.

"What a pity," Perfect crows, "that the choice of direction was not part of our arrangement. I think we'll be going north, and your team may go south."

I stare into Reaper's beaten eyes. I could probably force a real confession out of him, clear my name. But I've already strained Perfect's patience to the limit. If the truth came out, he'd slaughter me, my friends, and Reaper in front of all 250,000 viewers we've got watching us now.

"We done?" I make it a command.

"We're done."

I step back. Reaper hobbles away from the spikes and follows Perfect's crew down the northern tunnel.

Mischief hands me one of her enhanced healing potions. My satisfaction at beating Reaper pales before my rage at Perfect. "That rancid bastard," I curse between gulps. "He'll beat us to the boss for sure."

"I think not." Slayah manifests his parchment map. "The southern tunnel is our best bet."

I grin at him. "You lied?"

"I bluffed."

Heart claps Slayah on the back. "That's our tactician."

"Perfect won't be fooled for long." I set Not Today as my Flair and heft my mace. "Let's find the boss and dish out some retribution."

CHAPTER 25

A BRIDGE TO A DOOR

Heart, Mischief, Karma, Slayah, and I race down the southern tunnel. Within two minutes, I'm swatting aside cyborg spiders the size of golden retrievers.

"These bastards don't quit." Mischief hurls four of the small bombs she calls poppers. Ten spiders crawling along the walls burst apart, but two survive and land on Karma's back.

"Get them off! Get them off!" Karma spins but mashes her trigger. All six blunderbuss barrels fire as she twists and flails. I duck to avoid a headshot.

"Hold still, Karma." Heart glasses the spiders with quick burstblade thrusts. Red fragments cascade down Karma's muscly body.

"We must be nearing their nest." Slayah shoots a leaping spider from midair, spins, and clubs another sneaking up on him.

"Yeah," I agree, "their mobs are getting thicker."

Hissing little freaks rush at my knees in waves. It's all I can do to bludgeon them. I'm forced to dip into our dwindling antidote and potion supply as I take another bite.

Heart springs back to my side and helps carve away some of the monsters. One leaps at her, but I activate Not Today and take the damage. She stabs the spider to death.

"We must push through the swarm and complete our task." Slayah charges up his Flair and fires a lancing shot through a crowd of spiders. But a knot of the beasts surge up behind him.

"Slayah, watch out!" I rush to help him, but the spiders slash his health bar by a third before I reach him. Together, we swat the bugs into glass puddles.

"They are more dangerous in numbers," the archer observes.

"You think? Have a health potion, and keep your head on a swivel." Heart backs toward me. "We gotta fight back to back."

"That means slow going." I bang my mace on my shield in frustration. "But we don't have a choice. Slayah, are you sure the boss room is close?"

"Ninety-nine percent sure."

"Everyone form up," I call out. "Only use a potion if your health falls below half. Move!" I take point with Heart at my left and Karma on my right. Slayah and Mischief take the rear guard as we fight our way deeper into the dark.

"They finally stopped coming," Heart pants as she glasses the last spider.

Seeing that most of the party is hovering just above half health and we're down to three potions each dulls my relief. "Let's keep moving."

The tunnel widens into a circular cavern. Our path becomes a hundred-yard bridge spanning a cold abyss to a narrow landing. A flight of stairs rises from the landing to a pair of enormous redwood doors.

I slow to a stop and gawk at the doors. The gleaming ring handles set into the lacquered wood beckon me. "The boss room. We actually did it."

The rest of the party gathers around me. Slayah peers warily into the shadows. "I find it difficult to believe the boss room lies unguarded."

The chamber fills with skittering. A hundred spiders drop from the shadows above and land on the middle of the bridge. Worse, six hybrids with human upper bodies and spider lower bodies crawl down the walls. They brandish black scimitars and glare at us with blood-red eyes.

Mischief elbows Slayah. "You just had to say something, didn't you?"

I tighten my grasp on my mace. "We push toward the door. No stopping. Get to the boss room at any cost!"

The five of us charge the hundred spiders.

CHAPTER 26

HELPING HANDS

Heart and Mischief huddle behind my shield as we inch down the bridge. Their blades dart out and glass a handful of cyborg spiders. The monsters' pneumatic mandibles nibble away at our health.

Slayah and Karma slog along three paces behind us. They're too busy clubbing spiders to fire.

"They're biting my ankles!" Karma swings her gun like a club, smashing a half dozen spiders behind her and Slayah. But the tide of enemies fills in and continues draining their health bars.

Spiders leap at us from every angle. We struggle to form a circle. We're barely ten feet onto the bridge, but the doors at the far end might as well be on the moon.

"Who designed this room?" I shout over a cacophony of gnashing fangs.

"This swarm is excessive," Slayah yells back, "even for Cryoblend. It must be the Attendant AI!"

A spider leaps onto my back, and Rachel's winking face pops into my head. *Fixed that bug, my ass!*

Slayah bats the monster off me. "Relentless advance is unfeasible. Without a plan, we will perish at the threshold."

"You're the tactician, Slayah. Make it happen."

"I feared you would say that, Chains, because I see no way. If only we had more manpower . . ."

Why didn't I think of it before? I extend my shield's cover to Slayah, exposing myself. "Send a message to TacoKing. Tell him Chains needs him. I'm calling in the favor."

"That may suffice." Slayah presses his back against mine and slides open his window. His fingers dance across an invisible keyboard as monsters sink their fangs into my legs.

"Chains, here." Mischief shoves a potion into my hand. I chug it and refill my health bar from 30 percent to 80, but it instantly starts dropping again.

A spider centaur gallops at us. Its eight robot legs hold up a bloated black spider body topped by a human torso. The freak show raises a heavy scimitar in a double grip and swings at my head. I intercept the blow. The impact nearly tears the shield from my arm, but I activate the blade grabber. The centaur tries to yank his sword free to no effect.

"Heart," I call to the woman beside me, "disembowel him."

"I'm busy surviving here!" Heart slashes the dog-size spiders gnawing at her legs. She dances back from their dripping jaws and downs an antidote.

The spider centaur wrenches his blade free and swings again. I barely raise my shield in time to block the bone-jarring strike.

Slayah slides his window shut. "TacoKing is on his way. His team was already nearby." The archer nocks an arrow and shoots at the centaur. Its black sword bisects his arrow.

I swipe at the centaur's left front leg, but a spider jumps in the way and takes a glassing instead. "We need to hold out until they arrive."

"Correct. I suggest full defensive tactics until then."

"Everyone, you heard Slayah. Focus on surviving!"

"Don't breathe for a minute." Mischief hurls a vial of green liquid over my head and into the enemy ranks behind the centaur. The vial hits a spider and breaks. A green cloud of vapor smothers a dozen spiders, including the centaur. They all turn green and convulse as their health bars drain.

I lean away from the cloud and draw a breath. "You learned to make poison gas?"

"Why not? The Geneva Convention doesn't apply in video games."

Though poisoned, the spider centaur slips his sword under my guard and pierces Heart through the chest. She screams and falls off the blade. Her health dips to 20 percent.

"Close ranks on Heart!" I slam the centaur's blade aside, but he recovers and takes another stab at her. She screams as the sword enters her breast.

I activate Not Today and take the full damage. My health crashes to the dregs of my bar. "Karma, take over!"

"Gotcha, Chains!" The muscly mechanic shoulder-checks the centaur back into the mob. He stumbles and falls over, and she opens fire with her blunderbuss. The big guy finally takes a hit, and his five nearest allies get glassed.

I down a potion like a parched desert wanderer. Heart does the same. Our health bars ease back into the seventies. *Not many potions left between us.*

Mischief looks over our heads and freezes. "Oh, hell, no. That's too much."

I follow her gaze. Two more spider centaurs wade through the mob. The fallen monster climbs to its feet and joins its brethren pressing toward us.

"Chains, bro! We ca— What the hell?" TacoKing's voice rings out from behind us. "This is nuts. Red Rangers, charge!"

Five guys in bright red armor carve through the spiders mobbing the bridge between us and the tunnel mouth. TacoKing and his swinging battle-ax lead the way. TRexFromSpace and Chainsawlogy guard his right flank with their greatswords. **TurboCorndog** and **MaliciousDark**, two new guys in matching red armor, defend the left flank with two-handed mauls.

They're making good time, but the spider centaurs reach us first. I trap the first one's scimitar with my blade grabber and parry the second monster's sword with my mace. The third cuts Slayah across the chest.

He falls back and fires an arrow into its head. Each combatant loses a quarter of his health.

The spider centaur whose attack I parried rears back and kicks me. I fly backward but jerk to a stop with the first centaur's blade still trapped in my shield.

Mischief hurls a popper at the kicker's chest. The compact explosion melts half its health but fails to knock it down.

"Slayah, Heart, we aren't gonna make it this way. Siege Breaker time!" I angle my shield until it glows gold and slam it outward. A wave of light pushes all the enemies in front of me back. Heart flies past me and carves up their stumbling ranks with vicious swings. Slayah leaps over my head and fires ten arrows into the swarm.

Dozens of spiders die. One centaur explodes into glass. The other two shake off their injuries and raise their blades.

The five red warriors charge past me into the seething mob. I rally Retribution after them. Our combined party forms a wedge with me and Taco on point. Heart thrusts at the enemies that scrape my shield. Karma, Slayah, and Mischief stay inside the formation and finally get to focus on ranged offense.

"Chains," Taco shouts between slashes, "what's the deal here?"

"We gotta make it through those doors."

"Do they lead to—?"

"The boss room. Yeah."

"Chains, we're not ready, man. I say we get outta here."

I block a spider centaur's blade, let Chainsaw take over battling it, and turn to Taco. "You hate Perfect, right?"

"Dude's gutter slime. Why?"

"Perfect is the Copper Hoods' real leader. He and his crew will be here any minute. If he clears this boss, he'll be the hero of the server, and the Copper Hoods will merge with the Golden Dawn to form a giant fascist cult. This is our one chance to stop him."

Taco hacks a cyborg spider in half. "Damn. OK, then." He raises his voice over the din of battle. "Red Rangers, we're pushing with Chains and his buddies into the boss room. Gotta stop the Copper Hoods from getting the glory!"

"*All glory belongs to the emperor!*" Chainsaw rams his two-handed blade through the spider centaur's chest and cuts its health to zero. The giant monster explodes into a cloud of glass that cascades off his red armor.

TRex stomps a regular spider to death under his heavy boots. "Sounds like a chance for carnage. I'm in."

The five of us advance through the enemy ranks. It's slow going, but we reach the halfway point. I'm panting as I swing my mace for the thousandth time. "How are there still so many spiders?"

Slayah jerks a thumb over his shoulder. "Because they are filling in behind us."

I look back. More spiders scurry out from under the bridge. "Damn AI. A hundred spiders wasn't enough of a challenge?"

Slayah fires a cluster of arrows over my shoulder. "It is impossible to clear this chamber. I suggest we rush the doors."

I wave my mace around the enemy horde. "We'll get torn apart charging through this."

Mischief snorts. "We'll get torn apart slogging through this."

TacoKing whirls his battle-ax. "You know what they say. Faint heart never won bikini babe. We'll charge on your word."

I draw a deep breath. "Everyone make a break for the doors! Don't worry about kills; just clear a path and run!"

The five armored Rangers and I push forward. Spiders burst under our boots and fly from our kicks. The remaining spider centaurs slash at us as we run, and I take a glancing strike to the head that crushes my health. But we run on, heedless of the damage.

We arrive at the doors with every health bar below half, most in the bottom ten percent. The chattering mob at our backs boils forward to shred us.

"Push!" I ram my shoulder against the hard, smooth door and push with all my strength. The five Rangers join in. Karma and Mischief blow holes in the enemy ranks swarming our rear. Slayah shouts a command that's lost in the thunder of my pulse.

Heart presses against the lacquered redwood beside me and strains to force the doors. With a lurch, both massive portals open. The ten of us tumble into a world of blinding white light.

CHAPTER 27

DEATH

"I'm blind!" Heart shouts close beside me. I grope for her in the white void. When I find her silken fingers, she squeezes my hand.

"So am I," Mischief groans behind us, "but at least I can't read Slayah's name tag."

"Hold on." I squint into the glaring abyss. "I think it's just really bright. Give it a few seconds."

The white haze slowly fades to sapphire blue.

"Hey, it's the sky." Karma's tall, curvy form comes into focus. She spins around. "We're way up high."

"Of course we are, dummy," Mischief chides her. "We're on a mountaintop."

"No, Missy, I mean we're reeeally high."

"She's right. Look." I point to our right, where a sheer drop reveals the entire mountain range sprawling beneath us. The white marble walls of God's Staircase glimmer far below. "We're thousands of feet above the game world."

We stand on a broad disk floating in the sky. Elaborate tile designs cover the floor. A ring of stout marble pillars stands just inside the rim.

Heart brushes auburn hair out of her face. "This wind is nasty. And cold."

"Where is the boss?" Slayah's whole body is as taut as a guy wire. He nocks an arrow and scans the platform.

A wailing scream echoes from the mountains. Rhythmic pounding shakes the platform from below.

I chug my next-to-last healing potion and toss the empty vial into space. "Heal up and brace yourselves. Here comes the boss."

A twenty-foot clockwork spider leg rises over the pillars and crunches into the tiles. Three more legs appear. The platform groans as the robotic spider hauls itself up.

Heart gasps and takes a step back. "Chains, that thing is huge."

"I know. But we're gonna beat it."

Two clacking mandibles appear next. Gears whirr as the brass and steel construct climbs aboard.

The upper half of a woman's body sprouts from just behind the robot spider's head, and her pregnant belly rests upon it. Only a string bikini top covers her flawless blue flesh. Her long white hair streams in the wind.

"It's a composite of all the devs' kinks," Mischief deadpans.

TacoKing snorts. "Honestly, she'd be hot without the cyborg parts."

The spider queen gazes upon us with four glowing red eyes. She raises two black scimitars to the sky with another ethereal howl. The name **Kinnunra, Mother of Anguish** appears above her head, along with a health bar that looks ten miles long.

Slayah's eyes pore over the monster. "Her legs are tipped in blades. I see something orange swirling in her belly. Her second scream was not nearly equal in force to her first scream. Why?"

"Vanguard up front," I shout. "Rear guard, hang back until we see what she can do."

The five red guys form a wedge. I take my place beside TacoKing at the point. "How much do you trust your men?"

"Bruh, I got processed with TRex and Chainsaw. Corndog and Malicious joined up yesterday, but they're eager to prove themselves, you know?"

"They'd better be, Taco. Because the only way out of here is through spider Smurfette. We gotta hold the line."

Taco gives me a gauntleted fist bump. "I feel that, man."

Our wedge advances. When we hit the twenty yard line, Kinnunra creeps forward and spreads her two scimitars wide.

But instead of slashing at us, she draws a deep breath.

"Scatter!" Slayah shouts.

Kinnunra's pregnant belly glows from within, and she breathes a cone of fire. All ten of us dive in different directions.

TRex doesn't move fast enough. The roiling inferno engulfs him. His health bar drains to zero, and he bursts into green glass that sparkles in the conflagration.

"TRex!" TacoKing howls. "Damn you, Broadzilla!"

"In one hit?" The blood drains from Heart's face. "Just one hit?"

Kinnunra shuts her mouth, cutting off the flames. TRex's remains glitter on blackened tiles.

I point to the left and right. "Taco, half your men there, half on the other side. Rear guard, pair up with his teams. We need to form two fronts and spread our group."

TacoKing jabs a finger in my face. "Screw you, man. Your first order got TRex killed!"

The realization that a man died on my watch crashes down on me. My father's disappointed face emerges from my nightmares.

If only my son were a tenth of the man I needed him to be.

Slayah, Mischief, Karma, and Heart stand behind me, their eyes pleading for guidance. TacoKing and his men are scattered. He's so angry at me he hasn't issued new orders.

Kinnunra raises her right scimitar for a horizontal slash that will mow us all down.

What would Dad do? Doubts spin through my head, freezing me with indecision. "I can't save them, Dad. I'm not you!"

"Chains," Slayah says calmly, "you are not the man your father was. But you are my friend, and that is enough."

He's still with me. I failed him, hit him, but he still trusts me.

The need to protect my friends, no matter the risk, breaks my paralysis. I run forward with my shield raised and stop ten feet in front of Kinnunra. Her scimitar smashes into me with enough force to rattle my bones. The blow sends me skittering into a pillar and cuts my health by 30 percent.

As the boss pulls her blade back, I stand again and raise my shield high. "Guys, I can't stop her alone."

Kinnunra's blood-red eyes stare death at me.

I glare right back at death, no longer afraid.

The boss strikes again. An arrow flies from behind me. It bounces off Kinnunra's belly but stops her in midswing.

"Where would you be without your strategist?" says Slayah. "I shall always stand by your side."

Heart takes up a position at my right. "I'm with you, Chains."

Karma fires a blunderbuss volley into Kinnunra's spider body. The barrage shaves a sliver off the boss's health bar and sends her reeling. "First damage! Did you see that, Chains? One step closer to my crêpes."

Mischief steps to my left side. "You're gonna owe me more than crêpes for this."

The titan glares down at me, but my eye drifts to the viewer count in the corner of my vision as it hits one million. "Help me kill this blue bitch," I laugh, "and I'll pay whatever you want."

"Deal." Glowing orange vials sprout between Mischief's clenched fingers. She hurls all six at the boss. Kinnunra leaps back and craters the tiles underfoot as the bombs detonate in front of her.

I glance back at TacoKing, who's gathered his three surviving men. "We can mourn TRex later. Let's avenge him as a team."

Taco turns his black visor toward me. "If you're the man with the plan, I'll follow. Just don't consider us expendable."

"No life is expendable, Taco."

"Right." Taco faces his men. "Form two columns. We'll pincer this babe and cut her down to size!"

"Fire incoming," Slayah shouts.

Kinnunra draws a heavy breath. She aims right at my squad.

"Everyone break left!" I wait half a heartbeat to make sure everyone follows my order, then throw myself after them. Flames boil the tiles at my heels but miss us all. We form up again as the fire rages beside us.

"Time to get offensive. Mischief, hit her with some poppers."

Mischief hurls another handful of orange tubes at the boss. They explode against the spider's mechanical face. Kinnunra staggers.

Slayah and Karma pelt the boss with long-range attacks. Taco and Corndog rush her right side. Greatsword and maul clang on the spider's iron body and drain another few grains from her health bar.

Kinnunra turns to them and raises both scimitars.

Corndog presents his maul to the boss. "Chains blocked this attack. So can I!"

I reach helplessly for Corndog. "Wait, I only blocked one sword!"

Kinnunra slams both scimitars down. They smash through Corndog's maul, tear through his body, and bury themselves in the tiles.

Corndog's health bar plummets to zero. His jingling glass shards splash across the impact crater.

Everyone gawks, but I roar an order. "Hit her before she recovers!"

Slayah and Karma open fire. They barely do any damage. Taco screams Corndog's name as he slashes Kinnunra's legs. Explosions on the spider queen's back tell me Mischief's opened a can of judgment.

The rest of us charge the boss's back. Heart skewers the robot spider's main body. We eat 10 percent of Kinnunra's health bar. She draws herself fully upright and hefts her blades again.

Slayah waves his bow in the air. "Everyone fall back and prepare to dodge!" He nocks an arrow and squints up at Kinnunra.

I follow Slayah's line of sight. A gust of wind parts the white hair covering Kinnunra's forehead and displays a brilliant ruby set in her flesh like a third eye.

Mischief throws a popper. It bathes the ruby in flames. Kinnunra screams and rears up like a horse as her health plunges by 5 percent.

The spider queen lands with a crash and glares at Mischief. Her bottom jaw splits in half as she sucks in another breath.

"Dodge!" Slayah and I scream at the same time.

Instead of breathing fire, Kinnunra lets loose a piercing scream. It's the same wail that almost deafened us on arrival. My ears ache, my arms feel like noodles, and I stumble around drunkenly.

Text flashes across my screen: **Gained status effect Dazed.**

Kinnunra raises her left scimitar for another horizontal slash. Her four eyes lock onto Mischief wobbling beside me.

I'm weak as a kitten, but I can still shuffle. I knock down my nearest allies. Heart, Malicious, and Chainsaw flop to the tiles. I take another wobbling step toward Mischief as the sword closes on us. Her eyes bulge in terror, but she's shambling like a zombie. Grabbing her around the waist and raising my shield take all my diminished strength.

Kinnunra's blade crashes into my shield. Mischief and I roll across the platform like rag dolls. We crash into a column for additional damage, but I hold on to Mischief the whole way. The **Dazed** effect disappears.

Mischief's leather-clad body shakes in my arms. "You saved me."

"I'd do it again," I croak.

Mischief fishes two health potions from her pouch and hands one over. We both pop the stoppers and down them. I stand and haul her to her feet.

Kinnunra finishes her wide slash and returns her swords to high-ready position.

Mischief stares up at her. "Can we really win this?"

"Yes, if we hold together. Bomb her again and retreat out of her sword range." I raise my voice. "Slayah, Karma. Take turns with Mischief pummeling that red gem in the spider queen's forehead. The rest of you, only close in and hit her when she's finishing an attack and about to reset. Break off when she starts her next attack."

Kinnunra howls. The shadows of her dual scimitars fall on Mischief and me.

"Out of the way!" I grab Mischief's wrist and run. The two blades pulverize the column we'd been standing against.

"Now," I shout, "everyone hit her while her blades are down!"

Taco, Malicious, Chainsaw, Heart, and I smash Kinnunra with our melee weapons. Slayah, Karma, and Mischief pummel her with ranged attacks.

She's about to reset. "Slayah, hit her red gem!"

Slayah draws an arrow to his cheek. It blazes with blue light as he activates his Flair. The arrow leaves a dazzling sapphire trail as it nails Kinnunra's third eye. The hit rocks her back on her spider butt.

"Everyone get out of range and drop!" At my word, we scatter as Kinnunra rights herself and hinges her mouth open. All of us fall limp to the tiles.

Kinnunra swipes her right scimitar toward Slayah, Karma, and Malicious, but it sails harmlessly over their backs.

The Dazed effect passes, and we all climb to our feet. Kinnunra's health bar sits at 50 percent.

TacoKing pumps his fist. "We can do this!"

Kinnunra howls again, reverses her grip on her scimitars, and stabs them into the tiles. She leaves them standing erect as she sucks in a huge breath.

"Get back!" I raise my shield as the party backs away.

"Phase two." Slayah shelters behind one of the stone pillars ringing the platform. "Take cover. Fast!"

We all bolt to the edge of the platform as the spider queen releases her breath. Instead of one long line, she spins and blasts the whole disk with roiling flames. Fire washes over me before I can reach cover. The heat cooks me inside my armor.

I drag myself behind a pillar with just a sliver of my health left. As flames cascade over the platform's side and into empty air, I yank my last health potion from my belt and gulp it down.

The party health display shows me no one died, but everyone except Slayah and Karma took ridiculous damage.

I peek out from cover just as Kinnunra plucks up her scimitars and bounds at me with a vicious double swipe. I throw myself flat. Her swords scissor over my back and shear through the column. The top goes flipping toward the mountain range far below, leaving a two-foot stump.

I stand up and run. Kinnunra tracks me across the platform and chops both swords in vicious downward arcs. I barely roll out of the way. The impact vibrates the tiles.

Taco and Chainsaw charge Kinnunra's rump. She kicks her back legs like a horse. Their bladed tips seek the two warriors. Taco dodges. Chainsaw takes a brutal thrust to the chest and flies backward with a sliver of health left.

Kinnunra takes another swipe at me. I drop flat under the left scimitar and roll away from an overhead strike from the right.

"Karma, Mischief!" Slayah's voice rises above the raging battle. "Aim for Kinnunra's gem. She is moving fast, but you may get lucky. If she rears back, everyone run and drop."

Thunderclaps sound above my head. I barely get my shield up in time to block a scimitar chop. The boss's follow-up strike crashes into my side and leaves me with half health. I've got no potions left.

A boom splits the air, and Kinnunra rears back. Someone got lucky. I try to run but can't get away before she screams. The Dazed effect is even worse at close range. I can only stand there with locked knees and watch Kinnunra ready her right sword for a horizontal slash.

Karma tackles me to the ground. The blade grazes her as we fall, and she takes huge damage. The force of Kinnunra's attack spins her halfway around.

"You can't die, Chains." Karma shakes me. "You owe me dessert."

"You just earned yourself a lifetime supply." Dazed wears off, and we climb to our feet, barely alive.

Mischief runs up and presses healing potions into our hands, even though she's at 18 percent health. "Thank goodness you morons survived." Tears spring to her eyes. "I can't believe you idiots."

"Aw, Missy, I didn't mean—"

"Dodge!" Slayah screams.

Kinnunra sucks in a breath. Karma, Mischief, and I bolt for the nearest pillar and duck behind it. A wave of flame parts around it.

An arrow sprouts from Kinnunra's ruby. The boss pitches back.

"I can hit her even as she is recovering," Slayah says.

"Keep it up!" I urge him.

Kinnunra screams. We all wobble with the Dazed effect, but we're safe behind pillars. The boss's 360 slash hits no one. Her health is down to the last 10 percent.

Slayah draws another arrow, but Kinnunra arches her back and howls. Her blue flesh turns bright red. A second set of arms rips from her sides and plucks two more black scimitars from her clockwork spider body.

"Phase three!" Slayah cries.

Kinnunra's white hair stands on end. Her glowing eyes bulge with fury as she whirls her four curved blades in a maelstrom of death.

Slayah fires at Kinnunra's forehead, but she deflects his arrow. She lashes out with another blade spin and cleaves the pillar he'd hidden behind. The impact force reduces him to 5 percent health.

"Someone get Slayah a health potion!" I order.

"I gave you and Karma the last two!" Mischief cries.

I stare at Kinnunra's 90 percent depleted health bar as she completes her spin. Two projectile hits would kill her, but she's even blocking Karma's blunderbuss shots.

"Heart," I call to the swordswoman behind the pillar to my right. "Get ready to strike on my signal."

She smiles. "Will do."

"I'm going in," I tell the rest of my party. "Cover me."

Kinnunra rounds on us. I rush her. Taco, Malicious, and Chainsaw pass me. The boss aims a scimitar at each of them. They parry the three blades and go flying.

Slayah, Mischief, and Karma bombard Kinnunra's gem. The spider queen shields her face with her last sword, but the ruby is unguarded from below.

I rush in under the boss's nose. Her four eyes flick down to me. Three of her blades are still extended from attacking the Red Rangers. Her last blade hacks at me, but I catch it on my shield and press the handle trigger.

Enemy blade captured for 3 seconds.

Kinnunra retracts all four swords and lifts me skyward. As I dangle, I activate Meteor Rush. My shield radiates golden light. Heart hurtles past me. I swing my hips and push her foot with my stuck shield's edge. Heart rockets toward Kinnunra's face with her burstblade glowing gold.

She pierces the red gem, fires the gun barrels bracketing her blade, and goes streaking through the boss's head.

Kinnunra's health bar drains to zero. The spider queen gives one last piercing cry and blows apart in a hail of scarlet glass. Heart lands in a crouch at the platform's far edge.

Fireworks launched from the mountains below surround us with dazzling light. Post-battle text floods my vision, but a flashing window in my right eye distracts me.

The first floor dungeon boss has been defeated!
Death to Kinnunra, Mother of Anguish!
The killing combo was delivered by:
BrokenChains & HeartAtHome
And congratulations to the team who took her down:
AznMischief
Chainsawlogy
MaliciousDark
MechKarma
Pu$$y_$layah_666
TacoKing
RIP TRexFromSpace
RIP TurboCorndog

Our victory hasn't sunken in yet. My limbs are still shaking. My heart's still hammering.

I stare at the red glass covering the platform and whisper, "We made it."

"*We made it!*" Karma snatches Mischief and Heart up in a bear hug. They all laugh.

The Red Rangers stow their weapons. Taco puts a hand on Chainsawlogy's and MaliciousDark's shoulders. They nod solemnly.

Slayah jogs up to me. "I knew you would lead us to victory, Chains."

I raise my eyes from Kinnunra's remains to my friend's face. "I sure didn't."

Slayah meets my eyes and smiles. "You are your father's son after all."

I take a huge breath and feel like I exhale hot ashes. I'm lighter than before. "No, Slayah. I'd say I'm one-tenth of the man I need to be."

He scans my face. "Is one-tenth good?"

I smile. "It's enough."

Mischief interrupts the moment. "Our party's combined ratings are off the charts. Ten million people just watched us clean Kinnunra's clock."

My brain grinds to a halt. "Ten million?" I glance at my own streamer count. Five million.

"Yup," Mischief says, "and they're still watching. Anything you want to say to your adoring public?"

I stare up at the brilliant blue sky. Hope wells inside as I think of the mad payday the fight must have earned my family.

"Mom, Sis. I'm coming home. I'll cut my way out of this game and come back to you. Just hold on till I get there."

Heart stares up at the same spot. "Elizabeth, sweetie, Mommy hasn't forgotten you. Don't forget me. I'll be home soon!"

Everyone but Slayah and Mischief shout personal messages into the blue.

"Enough of the mushy stuff." I point at the eight loot bags among the evaporating glass, each tagged with a name. "Let's claim our rewards."

When each of us grabs a bag, the bright sky disappears. We're back underground in a circular chamber with torches ringing the stone walls. The massive redwood doors stand closed behind us.

A spiral staircase leads upward from the center of the room into the darkness high overhead.

Battered, exhausted, and drained of resources, the eight of us collect ourselves at the foot of the stairs.

But the moment my foot hits that first step, I'm humming with energy again. "Feels strange to say after we just barely survived, but I'm pumped. We really made it." I turn back to my crew. Seven pairs of eyes stare back at me with the same fire burning in my chest.

"We're gonna do it." Heart clenches her dainty fist at her breast. "We're really going home."

"Home is a ways off, but we proved today we have what it takes to bust out of this digital prison." I gesture at the staircase rising behind me. "Today we storm the second level. Then it's on to the third, the tenth, the twentieth, and eventually, the fiftieth. Nothing can stop us as long as we stick together and refuse to quit."

"Enough with the fancy speeches, stud. Let's see what floor two holds." Mischief shoos me up the steps.

The torchlight fades to black as we climb the seemingly endless steps. At last a speck of light appears and grows brighter as we ascend. After a few minutes that feel like hours, we emerge into a narrow stone chamber with a single door bearing a mural of Kinnunra. Inlaid rubies spell the words **Place hand here for entry, Champion.**

Heart and I exchange a glance and place our hands side by side on the mural. Stone shifts and grinds as the door rises out of sight. A hot breeze carrying the smell of sap and rain gusts in through the doorway. Somewhere, a flock of parrots squawk merrily in the sunlight.

We exit the door and descend a short flight of marble steps onto moist earth covered in vines and rubbery leaves.

"It appears to be a jungle." Slayah surveys the moist forest spread out before us. "I see temple ruins and groves of supertrees."

Far across the jungle, the second step of God's Staircase rises above the forest like a white cliff.

"We've got some levels to gain before we're ready for the next dungeon." I roll my shoulders and groan. "But first, I gotta sleep. Maybe for a week."

"There's your ride." Mischief points left to a bank of brass elevators in broad glass tubes. Their spinning gears flash in the sunlight. "Those should get us back down. Then it's a short walk to a hot meal."

Clattering footsteps draw my attention to the stone entry room. Perfect and his gang tromp into the sunlight. The would-be cult leader blinks in the harsh light until his eyes fall on me.

"You!" Perfect growls. "Do you have any idea what you've done?"

My crew falls in behind me. I let my shield rest in the dirt. "I opened the second floor. You're welcome."

"You deranged idiot." Perfect storms up to me and reaches for his sheathed sabers.

I forestall him with a raised hand. "Anything you want to say to the five million viewers watching my stream right now?"

Perfect drops his hands, but his glare is sharp enough to kill. "By stealing my accomplishment, you've undermined our greatest chance to unite as a people. Our server will splinter into competing factions. You may not like my methods, Chains, but you've doomed us all to a long march through this digital hell."

I jab a finger at him. "The people deserve a better leader than a poor man's Jim Jones. If we have to take the long way through this rat maze, at least we won't be your stepping-stones."

Perfect quivers with rage. "You cannot comprehend how many lives your actions will cost in the long run."

"And you don't get how much I hate petty tyrants like you. Now, either duel the server champion in front of five million viewers or get out of my face."

Perfect's face purples. His hands rise toward his saber hilts, but he spins and snarls at his crew. "Clear a path through this jungle. The next dungeon will be ours!"

The great dictator stalks into the trees with his guild hot on his heels. Rainpig and LaserToast sneer at me as they disappear into the foliage. Reaper lingers to meet my eyes before following the Knights.

"Good riddance," Mischief spits after them.

"Do you think they'll clear the next dungeon before us?" Heart asks me.

"Let them. We stole Perfect's glorious first boss kill. All we have to do is make sure he doesn't rack up a winning streak."

Mischief grins. "Devious. I like that."

Karma clutches her stomach. "Ooh, killing giant spider ladies is hungry work. I hear those crêpes down in Geartown calling my name."

"You've earned them." I pick up my shield and stride to the elevators but stop and look back at TacoKing and his two remaining men. "We couldn't have done this without you three. We're starting a guild. Want in?"

TacoKing rubs his helmet's chin. "We'd planned to make our own, but to tell you the truth, I'm not sure I'm cut out to lead. Losing TRex and Corndog really opened my eyes."

A pang of guilt darkens my spirits. "For what it's worth, I'm sorry about your men."

"No worries, Chains. Sorry about what I said. TRex's death wasn't your fault. He went into that battle knowing the risks. If you're leading, I'm joining. Can you open the guild yet?"

"In all the excitement, I forgot to check." I slide open my window and rock back on my heels. "Level eighty. That's a ton of experience points. I'll open the guild as soon as we get back to town."

TacoKing holds out his hand. "Righteous."

I clasp his hand and smile. "Glad to have you aboard. Let's ruin this prison."

The eight of us ride down the elevators. A good hundred Geartown citizens cluster around the new glass tubes built into the previously bare white cliff. They back away uncertainly as we exit, but then a few start clapping. By the time we're all standing on the stone steps outside the first dungeon, the whole crowd's applauding.

All I can do is stare.

Heart leans over to whisper, "Yesterday they spat on you. Today, you're their hero."

"People are disgustingly fickle," I say.

"You gave them hope," says Heart. "They trust you to get them home. That covers a lot of bad feelings."

The applause tapers off as adventurers flow past us to the row of elevators and glide up to the next floor.

We walk down the road to Geartown. When we arrive, the crowds part before us. No one spits at my feet. They aren't exactly throwing flowers before me, and a few people still sneer. But it's a start.

Mischief snorts. "Assholes. I wonder if this means we can shop again."

Heart snaps her fingers. "That reminds me. How's your shop doing?"

"Let me check." I open my menu again and switch over to my Merchant tab. My jaw drops. "Everything sold. We've got a fortune in here. And we haven't even checked our loot drops from the boss."

"I did. It was a compressed bag." Slayah slaps me on the back. "Each of us has gained a small fortune, plus various gear pieces and crafting items. Our group is now independently wealthy."

"Until we need to gear up for level two." TacoKing knocks on his breastplate. "We'll need better armor. And plenty of red paint."

"First, we need a house. I'm sick of inns." I gaze at Heart's smiling face. "Any street you'd like to live on?"

Her smile wilts. "I just want to get home. Elizabeth must be so scared without me."

"I'll get you back to her, Heart." I turn to my crew. "We'll all go home together." I raise my voice so the whole street can hear me. "I will get you home. I swear to all of you. No matter what it takes, I will free you from this digital hell!"

EPILOGUE

IN THE BLACK OF NIGHT . . .

At ten o'clock p.m. server time, a window opens in front of every player.

Trumpets blare.

Those already asleep are startled awake.

Those still fighting gape as their digital foes freeze in place.

Somewhere under a bridge, a serial killer with a poisoned blade flees as their sleeping intended victim wakes.

A slender blonde in a purple neon bikini appears in the window. Everyone recognizes Rachel Justice, California's Favorite Sentencing AI™. She waves at the audience with a cheerful laugh.

"Hello, all you wacky inmates. Hope you're having fun battling for survival. The administrative team wants me to deliver a special announcement. Stay tuned for the worst news of your digital lives!"

The view switches to a burning palace. Flames rage behind the blown-out windows.

Rachel appears in the bottom-right corner. She claps her hands to her cheeks in mock horror. "The vice president of the People's Republic of California has been assassinated! But don't worry. We caught the bomber." The burning palace screenwipes to a scene of ten guards in shiny chrome armor muscling a guy with a black bag over his head into the back of an armored transport. A few of them take turns punching him before the scene switches to a courtroom.

The fat hog of a judge slams his gavel on his podium. His jowls shake with rage. "A life sentence in God's Staircase. Let the machines kill him for us!"

"That's right, crime enthusiasts." Rachel's eyes sparkle with cartoon stars. "Our newest player is a real live terrorist. Hope you make him feel welcome. Don't be too harsh now, or he just might blow you up, too!"

She snaps her fingers. "I almost forgot. The administration has two personal messages for BrokenChains, who led his team to victory over Kinnunra, Mother of Anguish. First, the PRC Tax Service has withheld a Voluntary Community Compensation Donation from the funds you sent your family. The remainder should be enough to buy them a real meat dinner, if they share a plate.

"But there's more good news. We're sending you a new friend!"

The screen star wipes to a still shot of a scruffy convict covered with stubble. His gaping mouth and flaring nostrils indicate they snapped the shot as he screamed at the camera.

Rachel pops up to whisper behind her hand. "Hey, Chains. Remember the guy you killed? Of course you do! His brother is looking for you. He robbed a bank and sat waiting to get arrested. His only request at sentencing was to be placed on your server. Your judge happily obliged him."

The still unfreezes. Spittle hits the lens, distorting the picture. "You're dead, Donovan," the robber yells. His bloodshot eyes bulge as he screams. "Do you hear me, killer? I'm coming to gut you for what you did to my brother. I'll see you *real soon*!"

To be continued in *Level Up or Die*, Volume 2.

CONTINUE THE ADVENTURE

Be the first to hear about *Level Up or Die*, Volume 2 and other novels, nonfiction, short stories, and courses by Joshua Lisec and Adam Lane Smith. Here's how.

- Subscribe to Joshua and Adam's literary newsletter at www. LisecAndSmithBooks.com.
- Visit Joshua's website at www.EntrepreneursWordsmith.com.
- Check out Adam's blog at www.AdamLaneSmith.com.
- Follow Joshua (@JoshuaLisec) and Adam (@TheBrometheus) on Twitter.

Introducing *The 80/20 Fiction System*

Write a Great Novel Faster Than You Ever Thought Possible

The novel you just read was produced using Joshua Lisec and Adam Lane Smith's *80/20 Fiction System*. Crafted from years of experience writing a combined total of 80 books, this program leverages the 80/20 Principle so you invest time on only activities that produce a commercially viable book — and none on activities that don't.

If you've always wanted to write a novel, or if you're an author looking to crank your productivity into overdrive, check out Joshua and Adam's fiction writing masterclass at **www.8020FictionSystem.com**.

ACKNOWLEDGEMENTS

Producing a book is a team effort. Especially a book as epic as this one. The authors would like to thank each and every person who contributed to this experience.

Thanks also to the team of artists who helped design our cover. We never knew a clockwork shield could look so cool.

Shout out to all our followers scattered across social media for spreading the word and sharing your enthusiasm during the writing and launch. Your incredible energy convinced us there's space on the shelf for a story about prisoners playing video games. We hope to entertain you for many years to come as *Level Up or Die* expands well beyond this first novel.

And thank you to our loving wives. We authors pound away at the keys all day to complete these books, but that labor is only possible because our partners hold up the rest of our lives. Thank you for your dedication and unfailing patience in helping us provide for our families.

And a hearty thanks to you, dear reader, for sticking with us. We hope you join us again for the next volume. Until then, don't let any cyborg spider queens get you down.

See you soon.

ABOUT THE AUTHORS

Joshua Lisec, www.EntrepreneursWordsmith.com

Joshua Lisec is the world's only award-winning, celebrity-recom-mended, #1 international bestselling Certified Professional Ghostwriter. Joshua has ghostwritten more than 60 full-length books and has copy-written thousands of articles, emails, proposals, and sales pages for clients in over 100 industries.

Joshua is the creator of the bestselling *The Best Way* courses, including *The Best Way To Say It*, used by thousands worldwide to improve their persuasive writing skills. He is also a TEDx Speaker and co-creator of *The 80/20 Fiction System* with Adam Lane Smith. Use Joshua's free tools for nonfiction authors, including a book launch revenue calcula-tor, at www.EntrepreneursWordsmith.com. Follow him on Twitter @ JoshuaLisec.

Adam Lane Smith, www.AdamLaneSmith.com

Adam Lane Smith is a two-time #1 Amazon bestselling novelist and a licensed psychotherapist specializing in trauma and attachment with experience in both clinical and correctional mental health settings. That includes his work in the California justice system where he treated inmates facing the death penalty.

Adam has written 20 books and coached over 500 aspiring novelists through his program *Write Like a Beast*. He is also the co-creator of *The 80/20 Fiction System* with Joshua Lisec. Adam's attachment treatment method detailed in his book *Slaying Your Fear* is used by mental health professionals across the US, and he has delivered seminars instructing healthcare professionals in treating patients with attachment concerns. Download Adam's book *Brothers to the End* for free at www. AdamLaneSmith.com. Follow him on Twitter @TheBrometheus.